*Praise for Charles Yu's*

# Sorry
# Please
# Thank You

D0963396

"There's some of the cerebral gamesmanship of Jonathan Lethem, the resigned sadness of Kurt Vonnegut, the Phil Dickian paranoiac distrust of consumer culture. But Yu's voice, sensibility and approach are unique. . . . The stories deliver more than their fair share of bitter laughs, philosophical conundrums and existential gut punches." —*San Francisco Chronicle*

"Mind-bending, moving and sometimes melancholy stories." —CNN.com

"Lovely and heartfelt. . . . A brilliantly manic ride. . . . Yu has an undeniable gift for describing, in clean, economical prose, the mechanics of things that don't exist or are impossible."

—*The Wall Street Journal*

"Terrific reading for the heart as well as the head."

—*All Things Considered*, NPR

"Entertaining. . . . Like a friend who stops by unexpectedly with a bunch of mind-bending tales to share. . . . Had me laughing. . . . Go order a copy."
—Geek Dad, *Wired* magazine

"Laugh-out-loud moments of strangeness artfully exist in a contemporary fictional structure. . . . With this collection, steeped in originality, we get echoes of David Foster Wallace's early collection, *Girl with the Curious Hair*. Like Wallace, Yu abandons the more self-serving, insular metafiction of the past forty years for a fresher form."     —*Paste* magazine

"Grade A-. . . . Pick it up and kiss your weekend goodbye."                                          —*The Boston Phoenix*

"In his new collection, Charles Yu applies his trademark winking, pop-culture-infused, sci-fi mentality to a series of short stories. . . . Clever and cutting."
—*Flavorwire*

"Whether Yu's work is dark, thought provoking, humorous, or all of the above, it's always compulsively readable."                          —Owl and Bear.com

"[Charles Yu is] the computer century's heir to Philip K. Dick and Ray Bradbury."       —*Shelf Awareness*

Charles Yu

# Sorry
# Please
# Thank You

Charles Yu is the author of *How to Live Safely in a Science Fictional Universe*, which was named one of the best books of the year by *Time* magazine. He received the National Book Foundation's 5 Under 35 Award for his story collection *Third Class Superhero*, and was a finalist for the PEN Center USA Literary Award. His work has been published in *The New York Times*, *Playboy*, and *Slate*, among other periodicals. Yu lives in Los Angeles with his wife, Michelle, and their two children.

Also by Charles Yu

*Third Class Superhero*
*How to Live Safely in a Science Fictional Universe*

☐ Sorry

☐ Please

☐ Thank You

☑ Sorry

☑ Please

☑ Thank You

☐ Charles Yu

Vintage Contemporaries

Vintage Books

A Division of Random House, Inc. I New York

FIRST VINTAGE CONTEMPORARIES EDITION, MAY 2013

Portions of this work were originally published in the following:
"Sorry Please Thank You" on Esquire.com; "Open" in *Explosion-Proof*;
"Designer Emotion 67" in *The Oxford American*; "Yeoman" in *Playboy*;
"First Person Shooter" on Wired.com/Geek Dad; "Standard Loneliness
Package" in *Lightspeed Magazine* and reprinted in *The Year's Best
Science Fiction & Fantasy, 2011 Edition*, edited by Richard Horton
(Gaithersburg, MD: Prime Books, 2011); and "The Book of Categories"
in *The Thackery T. Lambshead Cabinet of Curiosities*, edited by Jeff and
Ann Vandermeer (New York: Harper Voyager, 2011).

The Library of Congress has cataloged the Pantheon edition as follows:
Yu, Charles.
Sorry please thank you : stories / Charles Yu.
p. cm.
I. Title.
PS3625.U15S67 2012
813'.6—dc23 2011049487

Vintage ISBN: 978-0-307-94846-5

Book design by Michael Collica

www.vintagebooks.com

Printed in the United States of America
10  9  8  7  6  5  4  3  2

For Kelvin. Hey man.

Human beings do not live in the objective world alone . . . but are very much at the mercy of the particular language which has become the medium of expression for their society. . . . The fact of the matter is that the "real world" is to a large extent unconsciously built upon the language habits of the group. No two languages are ever sufficiently similar to be considered as representing the same social reality.

—Edward Sapir

We dissect nature along lines laid down by our native languages.

—Benjamin Lee Whorf

Sorry.

—Anonymous

 Sorry

# Standard Loneliness Package

Root canal is one fifty, give or take, depending on who's doing it to you. A migraine is two hundred.

Not that I get the money. The company gets it. What I get is twelve dollars an hour, plus reimbursement for painkillers. Not that they work.

I feel pain for money. Other people's pain. Physical, emotional, you name it.

Pain is an illusion, I know, and so is time, I know, I know. I know. The shift manager never stops reminding us. Doesn't help, actually. Doesn't help when you are on your third broken leg of the day.

I get to work three minutes late and already there are nine tickets in my inbox. I close my eyes, take a deep breath, open the first ticket of the morning:

I'm at a funeral.

Feeling grief.

Someone else's grief. Like wearing a stranger's coat, still warm with heat from another body.

I'm feeling a mixture of things.

Grief, mostly, but also I detect some guilt in there. There usually is.

I hear crying.

I am seeing crying faces. Pretty faces. Crying, pretty, white faces. Nice clothes.

Our services aren't cheap. As the shift manager is always reminding us. *Need I remind you?* That is his favorite phrase these days. He is always walking up and down the aisle tilting his head into our cubicles and saying it. *Need I remind you,* he says, *of where we are on the spectrum?* In terms of low-end high-end? We are solidly toward the highish end. So the faces are usually pretty, the clothes are usually nice. The people are usually nice, too. Although I imagine it's not such a big deal to be nice when you're that rich and that pretty.

There's a place in Hyderabad doing what we're doing, but a little more toward the budget end of things. Precision Living Solutions, it's called. And of course there are hundreds of emotional engineering firms here in Bangalore, springing up everywhere you look. The other day I read in the paper that a new call center opens once every three weeks. Workers follow the work, and the work is here. All of us ready to feel, to suffer. We're in a growth industry.

Okay. The body is going into the ground now. The crying is getting more serious.

Here it comes.

I am feeling that feeling. The one that these people get a lot, near the end of a funeral service. These sad and pretty people. It's a big feeling. Different operators have different ways to describe it. For me, it feels something like a huge boot. Huge, like it fills up the whole sky, the whole galaxy, all of space. Some kind of infinite foot. And it's stepping on me. The infinite foot is stepping on my chest.

The funeral ends, and the foot is still on me, and it is hard to breathe. People are getting into black town cars. I also appear to have a town car. I get in. The foot, the foot. So heavy. Here we go, yes, this is familiar, the foot, yes, the foot. It doesn't hurt, exactly. It's not what I would call comfortable, but it's not pain, either. More like pressure. Deepak, who used to be in the next cubicle, once told me that this feeling I call the infinite foot—to him it felt more like a knee—is actually the American experience of the Christian God.

"Are you sure it is the Christian God?" I asked him. "I always thought God was Jewish."

"You're an idiot," he said. "It's the same guy. Duh. The Judeo-Christian God."

"Are you sure?" I said.

He just shook his head at me. We'd had this conversation before. I figured he was probably right, but I didn't want to admit it. Deepak was the smartest guy in our cube-cluster, as he would kindly remind me several times a day.

I endure a few more minutes of the foot, and then, right before the hour is up, right when the grief and guilt are almost too much and I wonder if I am going to have to hit the safety button, there it is, it's usually there at the end of a funeral, no matter how awful, no matter how hard I am crying, no matter how much guilt my client has saved up for me to feel. You wouldn't expect it—I didn't—but anyone who has done this job for long enough knows what I'm talking about, and even though you know it's coming, even though you are, in fact, waiting for it, when it comes, it is always still a shock.

Relief.

Death of a cousin is five hundred. Death of a sibling is twelve fifty. Parents are two thousand apiece, but depending on the situation people will pay all kinds of money, for all kinds of reasons, for bad reasons, for no reason at all.

The company started off in run-of-the-mill corporate services, basic stuff: ethical qualm transference, plausible deniability. The sort of things that generated good cash flow, cash flow that was fed right back into R&D, year after year, turning the little shop into a bit player, and then a not-so-bit player, and then, eventually, into a leader in a specialized market. In those early days, this place was known as Conscience Incorporated. The company had cornered the early market in guilt.

Then the technology improved. Some genius in Delhi had figured out a transfer protocol to standardize and packetize all different kinds of experiences. Overnight, everything changed. An industry was born. The business of bad feeling. For the right price, almost any part of life could be avoided.

Across the street from work is a lunch place I go to sometimes. Not much, really, a hot and crowded little room, a bunch of stools in front of a greasy counter. I come here mostly for the small television, up on a shelf, above the cash register. They have a satellite feed.

Today they have it switched to American television, and I am watching a commercial for our company's services.

It shows a rich executive-looking type sitting and rubbing his temples, making the universal television face for I Am an Executive in a Highly Stressful Situation. There are wavy lines on either side of his temples to indicate that the Executive is really stressed! Then he places a call to his broker and in the next scene, the Executive is lying on a beach, drinking golden beer from a bottle and looking at the bluest ocean I have ever seen.

Next to me is a woman and her daughter. The girl, maybe four or five, is scooping rice and peas into her mouth a little at a time. She is watching the commercial in silence. When she sees the water, she turns to her mother and asks her, softly, what the blue liquid is. I am thinking about how sad it is that she has never seen water that color in real life until I realize that I am thirty-nine years old and hey, you know what? Neither have I.

And then the commercial ends with one of our slogans.
*Don't feel like having a bad day?*
*Let someone else have it for you.*

That someone else they are talking about in the commercial is me. And the other six hundred terminal operators in Building D, Cubicle Block 4. Don't feel like having a bad day? Let me have it for you.

It's okay for me. It's a good job. I didn't do that well in school, after all. It was tougher for Deep. He did three semesters at technical college. He was always saying he deserved better. Better than this, anyway. I would nod and agree with him, but I never told him what I wanted to tell him, which was, hey, Deepak, when you say that you deserve better, even if I agree with you, you are kind of also implying that I don't deserve better, which, maybe I don't, maybe this is about where I belong in the grand scheme of things, in terms of high-end low-end for me as a person, but I wish you wouldn't say it because whenever you do, it makes me feel a sharp bit of sadness and then, for the rest of the day, a kind of low-grade crumminess.

Whenever Deep and I used to go to lunch, he would try to explain to me how it works.

"Okay, so, the clients," he would say, "they call in to their account reps and book the time."

He liked to start sentences with okay, so. It was a habit he had picked up from the engineers. He thought it made him sound smarter, thought it made him sound like them, those code jockeys, standing by the coffee machine, talking faster than he could think, talking not so much in sentences as in data structures, dense clumps of logic with the

8

occasional inside joke. He liked to stand near them, pretending to stir sugar into his coffee, listening in on them as if they were speaking a different language. A language of knowing something, a language of being an expert at something. A language of being something more than an hourly unit.

Okay, so, Deepak said, so this is how it works. The client, he books the time, and then at the appointed hour, a switch in the implant chip kicks on and starts transferring his consciousness over. Perceptions, sensory data, all of it. It goes first to an intermediate server where it gets bundled with other jobs, and then a huge block of the stuff gets zapped over here, downloaded onto our servers, and then dumped into our queue management system, which parcels out the individual jobs to all of us in the cubicle farm.

Okay, so, it's all based on some kind of efficiency algorithm—our historical performance, our current emotional load. Sensors in our head assembly unit measure our stress levels, sweat composition, to see what we can handle. Okay? he would say, when he was done. Like a professor. He wanted so badly to be an expert at something.

I always appreciated Deepak trying to help me understand. But it's just a job, I would say. I never really understood why Deep thought so much of those programmers, either. In the end, we're all brains for hire. Mental space for rent, moments as a commodity. They have gotten it down to a science. How much a human being can take in a given twelve-hour shift. Grief, embarrassment, humiliation, all different, of course, so they calibrate our schedules, mix it up, the timing and the order, and the end result is you leave work every day right about at your exact breaking point. I used to smoke to take the edge off, but I quit twelve years ago, so sometimes when I get home, I'm still shaking for a little bit. I sit on my couch and drink a beer and let it subside. Then I heat up some bread and lentils and read a newspaper or, if it's too hot to stay in, go down to the street and eat my dinner standing there, watching people walking down the block, wondering where they are headed, wondering if anyone is waiting for them to come home.

When I get to work the next morning, there's a woman sitting in the cubicle across from mine. She's young, at least a couple of years younger than me, looks right out of school. She has the new-employee setup kit laid out in front of her and is reading the trainee handbook. I think about saying hi but who am I kidding, I am still me, so instead I just say nothing.

My first ticket of the day is a deathbed. Deathbeds are not so common. They are hard to schedule—we require at least twenty-four hours' advance booking, and usually clients don't know far enough in advance when the ailing loved one is going to go. But this isn't regular deathbed. It's pull-the-plug.

They are pulling the plug on Grandpa this morning.

I open the ticket.

I am holding Grandpa's hand.

I cry.

He squeezes my hand, one last burst of strength. It hurts. Then his hand goes limp.

I cry, and also, I really cry. Meaning, not just as my client, but I start crying, too. Sometimes it happens. I don't know why, exactly. Maybe because he was somebody's grandpa. And he looked like a nice one, a nice man. Maybe something about the way his arm fell against the guardrail on the hospital bed, nothing dramatic or poignant. Just a part of his body going thunk against metal. Maybe because I could sort of tell, when Grandpa was looking at his grandson for the last time, looking into his eyes, looking around in there trying to find him, he didn't find him, he found me instead, and he knew what had happened, and he didn't even look mad. Just hurt.

I am at a funeral.

I am in a dentist's chair.

I am lying next to someone's husband in a motel bed, feeling guilty.

I am quitting my job. This is a popular one. Clients like to avoid the awkwardness of quitting their jobs, so they set an appointment and walk into their bosses' offices and tell them where they can stick this effing job, and right before the boss starts to reply, the switch kicks in and I get yelled at.

I am in a hospital.

My lungs burn.

My heart aches.

I'm on a bridge.

My heart aches on a bridge.

My heart aches on a cruise ship.

My heart aches on an airplane, taking off at night.

Some people think it's not so great that we can do this. Personally, I don't really see the problem. Press one to clear your conscience. Press two for fear of death. Consciousness is like anything else. I'm sure when someone figures out how to sell time itself, they'll have infomercials for that, too.

I am at a funeral.

I am losing someone to cancer.

I am coping with something vague.

I am at a funeral.

I am at a funeral.

I am at a funeral.

Seventeen tickets today in twelve hours. Ten half hours and seven full.

On my way out, I can hear someone wailing and gnashing his teeth in his cubicle. He is near the edge. Deepak was always like that, too. I always told him, hey man, you have to let go a little. Just a little. Don't let it get to you so much.

I peek my head to see if I can steal a glance at the new woman, but she is in the middle of a ticket. She appears to be suffering. She catches me looking at her. I look at my feet and keep shuffling past.

It used to be that the job wasn't all pain. Rich American man outsources the nasty bits of his life. He's required to book by the hour or the day or some other time unit, but in almost any crappy day, there are always going to be some parts of it that are not so bad. Maybe just boring. Maybe even more okay than not. Like if a guy books his colonoscopy and he hires us for two hours, but for the first eight minutes, he's just sitting there in the waiting room, reading a magazine, enjoying the air-conditioning, admiring someone's legs. Or something. Anyway, it used to be that we would get the whole thing, so part of my job here could be boring or neutral or even sometimes kind of interesting.

But then the technology improved again and the packeting software was refined to filter out those intervals and collect them. Those bits, the extras, the leftover slices of life were lopped off by the algorithm and smushed all together into a kind of reconstituted life slab, a life-loaf. Lunch meat made out of bits of boredom. They take the slabs and process them and sell them as prepackaged lives.

I've had my eye on one for a while, at a secondhand shop that's on my way home. Not ideal, but it's something to work for.

So now, what's left over is pretty much just pure undiluted badness. The only thing left to look forward to is when, once in a while, in the middle of an awful day, there is something not-so-awful mixed in there. Like the relief in the middle of a funeral, or sometimes when you get someone who is really religious, not just religious, but a person of true faith, then mixed in with the sadness and loss you get something extra, you get to try different flavors, depending on the believer. You get the big foot on your chest, or you get the back of your head on fire, a cold fire, it tickles. You get to know what it is like to know that your dead lover, your dead mother, father, brother, sister, that they are all standing in front of you, tall as the universe, and they have huge, infinite feet, and their heads are all ablaze with this brilliant, frozen fire. You get the feeling of being inside of a room and at the same time, the room being inside of you, and the room is the world, and so are you.

The next day is more of the same. Eleven tickets. The low-light of the day is when I get to confess to my husband that I have been sleeping with my trainer for the last year. The first year of our marriage. I get to see his face, watch him try to keep it together. Of all the types of tickets, this is the worst. Heartbreak. When I first started at this job, I thought physical pain would be hardest. But it's not. This is the hardest. To be inside here, looking at this man's face, at the lowest moment of his life, watching him try to keep it together. To be inside here, feeling what this woman is feeling, having done this to him. And then the world blinks twice and my field of vision goes blue and I'm a guy sitting in front of a computer screen and the sandwich cart is in front of my cubicle.

So I have lunch.

After lunch, I pass her in the hall. The new woman. Her name badge says Kirthi. She doesn't look at me this time.

On the way home from work, I decide to swing by the secondhand shop and check out my life.

It's not my life, technically. Not yet. It's the life I want, the life I've been saving for. Not a DreamLife®, not top of the line, but a starter model, a good one. Standard possibility. Low volatility. A kindhearted wife with nice hair, 0.35 kids, no actuals, certainties are too expensive, but some potential kids, a solid thirty-five percent chance of having one. Normal life expectancy, average health, median aggregate amount of happiness. I test-drove it once, and it felt good, it felt right. It fit just fine.

I don't know. I'm trying not to feel sorry for myself. I just thought there might be more to it all than this.

Still, I've got it better than some people. I mean, I'm renting my life out one day at a time, but I haven't sold it yet. And I don't plan to, either. I'm buying in, not selling out. I want to live, not exist, want to have a life, even if it is bits and pieces, even if it isn't the greatest product out there, even if it's more like a life-substitute. I'll take it.

I'm not going to be like my father, who sold his life on a cold, clear afternoon in November. He was thirty. It was the day before my fourth birthday.

We went to the brokerage. It felt like a bank, but friendlier. My father had been carrying me on his shoulders, but he put me down when we got inside. There was dark wood everywhere, and also bright flowers and classical music. We were shown to a desk, and a woman in an immaculate pantsuit asked if we would like anything to drink. My father didn't say anything, just looked off at the far wall. I remember my mother asked for a cup of tea for my father.

I don't want to sell my life. I'm not ready to do that yet. So I sell it bit by bit. Scrape by. Sell it by the hour. Pain, grief, terror, worse. Or just mild discomfort. Social anxiety. Boredom.

I ask around about Kirthi. People are talking. The guys are talking. Especially the married guys. They do the most talking.

I pass her in the hall again, and again she doesn't look at me. No surprise there. Women never look at me. I am not handsome or tall. But I am nice.

I think it is actually that which causes the not-looking at me. The niceness, I mean, not the lack of handsomeness or tallness. They can see the niceness and it is the kind of niceness that, in a man, you instinctively ignore. What is nice? What good is a nice man? No good to women. No good to other men.

She doesn't look at me, but I feel, or maybe I wish or I imagine, that something in the way she does not look at me is not quite the same. She is not-looking at me in a way that feels like she is consciously not-looking at me. And from the way she is not-looking at me, I can tell she knows I am trying to not-look at her. We are both not-looking at each other. And yet, there is something in the way she is not-looking at me. For the first time in a long while, I have hope.

I am at a funeral. Again.

I'm flipped to green.

You can be flipped to green, or flipped to red.

You can be there, or can just feel the feeling.

This is the one improvement they have made that actually benefits us workers. There's a toggle switch on the headset. Flip it to green and you get a rendering of the client's visual field. You see what he sees. Flip it to red and you still feel all of the feelings, but you see what you see.

You can do whatever you want, so long as you don't leave your cubicle. Some people just stare at the cube-divider wall. Some play computer solitaire. Some even chat with neighbors, although that is strongly discouraged.

I was hesitant at first, but more and more these days I am usually flipped to red. Except for funerals. Funerals, I like to be there, just out of some kind of respect thing.

This morning's first ticket: sixtyish rich guy, heart attack in the home office, millions in the bank, five kids from three marriages, all hate him.

Client is one of those kids, trust-fund baby, paid extra for amnesia. No feeling, no pre-feeling, no hangover, no residue, no chance of actually having any part of it, long enough to ensure that he will be halfway in the bag before any of the day's events start nibbling at the corners of his awareness.

I see the fresh, open plot. A little rain falls on the funeral procession as they get out of the cars, but there's a break in the clouds so that it's raining and the sun is shining at the same time.

As usual, everyone is well dressed. A lot of the rich look mildly betrayed in the face of death, as if they are a little bit surprised that good style and a lot of money weren't quite enough to protect them from the unpleasantness of it all. I'm standing next to what I am guessing is widow number two, late thirties, probably, with beautiful sand-colored hair. We make eye contact and she is staring at me and I am trying not to stare at her and then we both realize the same thing at the same time. Raj, I almost say, catching myself before I do, but something in my eyes must give it away anyway, because she smiles, or he smiles. I'm not quite sure which one smiles, Raj, or the person he is hiding inside of.

Rajiv usually works night shift now, so I haven't seen him in a while. He must have picked up a day shift. We used to have a beer or two after work. A friend, I would call him. I want to call him that. One of the few I've had in this line of work.

The pastor talks about a full life lived, and the limits of earthly rewards, and everyone nods affirmatively, and then there is music as the body goes into the ground, I've heard it at a lot of funerals. Mozart, I think, but I am not sure. Sometimes I think that's really what my job is. Nodding and crying and listening to Mozart. And I think, there are worse things. There are.

Death of an aunt is seven hundred. Death of an uncle is six.

Bad day in the markets is a thousand. Kid's recital is one twenty-five an hour. Church is one fifty.

The only category that we will not quote a price on is death of a child. Death of a child is separately negotiated. Hardly anyone can afford it. And not all operators can handle it. We have to be specially trained to be eligible for those tickets. People go on sick leave, disability. Most people just physically cannot do it. There hasn't been one booked the whole time I've been here, so most of us aren't even sure what is true and what isn't. The rumor is that if you do one, you are allowed to take the rest of the month off. Deep was always tempted. It's not worth it, I would tell him. Okay, so, maybe not for you, Deep said. Okay, so, mind your own business, he would say.

The first time I talk to Kirthi is by the water fountain. I tell her we are neighbors, cubicle-wise. She says she knows. I feel a bit stupid.

The second time we talk, we are also by the water fountain, and I try to say something charming, we have to stop meeting like this or something terrible like that. I probably saw it on TV and it just came out. Stupid. She doesn't laugh, but she doesn't frown, either. She just kind of looks at me, as if trying to figure out how I could have thought that was a good idea.

The third time we talk, I kiss her. By the microwave in the snack room. I don't know what got into me. I am not an aggressive person. I am not physically strong. I weigh one hundred and forty-five pounds. She doesn't laugh. She actually makes a face like disgust. But she doesn't push me away, either. Not right away. She accepts the kiss, doesn't kiss back, but after a couple of seconds, breaks it off and leans back and turns her head and says, under her breath, You shouldn't have done that.

Still, I am happy. I've got three more tickets in the bucket before lunch, and then probably eight or nine before I go home, but the whole rest of the day, I am having an out-of-my-body experience. Even when I am in someone else's body, I am still out of my body.

I weep.

I wail.

I gnash my teeth.

Underneath it all, I am smiling.

I am at a funeral. My client's heart aches, and inside of it is my heart, not aching, the opposite, doing that, whatever it is. My heart is doing the opposite of aching.

□

Kirthi and I start dating. That's what I call it. She calls it letting me walk her to the bus stop. She lets me buy her lunch. She tells me I should stop. She still never smiles at me.

I'm a heartbreak specialist, she says.

When I see her in the hallway, I walk up behind her and slip my arm around her waist.

She has not let me in yet. She won't let me in.

Why won't you let me in? I ask her.

You don't want in, she says. You want around. You want near. You don't want in.

There are two hundred forty-seven ways to have your heart broken, she says, and I have felt them all.

I am in a hospice.

I have been here before. A regular client.

I am holding a pen.

I have just written something on a notepad in front of me.

My husband is gone.

He died years ago.

Today is the tenth anniversary of his death.

I have Alzheimer's, I think.

A memory of my husband surfaces, like a white-hot August afternoon, resurfacing in the cool water of November.

I tear off the sheet of paper.

I read it to myself.

It is a suicide note.

I raise a glass to my mouth, swallow a pill. Catch a glance of my note to the world.

The fail-safe kicks on, the system overrides. I close the ticket. I'm out just in time, but as I leave this dying mind,

I feel the consciousness losing its structure. Not closing down. Opening. As it dies, I feel it opening up, like a box whose walls fall away, or a maybe a flowering plant, turning toward the sun.

Kirthi hasn't been to work for the past two days.

It's her father.

That's what Sunil tells me, one day over a beer.

Kirthi's father is still mortgaged, Sunil explains. Locked in. Sold his life. "Just like yours," Sunil says. "Right?"

I nod.

Sunil is in tech support, so he's seen all of the glitches. He knows what can go wrong in the mechanics of feeling transfers. Sunil has seen some strange things.

"There's no upper bound on weird," he says.

"This is going to end badly, man," he says. "You have to trust me on this. Kirthi is damaged. And she knows it."

Sunil means well, but what he doesn't know is that I am fine with damaged. I want damage. I've looked down the road I'm on and I see what's coming. A lot of nothing. No great loves lost. And yet, I feel like I lost something. Better to have loved and lost than never to have loved at all? How about this: I lost without the love. I've lost things I've never even had. A whole life.

But as the weeks go on, I begin to think Sunil might be right.

"Kirthi won't let me in," I tell him. "She tells me to get away from her, to run."

"She is doing you a favor, man. Take her advice."

I ask her about her father.

She doesn't talk to me for a week.

And then, on Friday night, after we walk for an hour in silence, before going into her apartment, she turns to me. "It's awful," she says. "To see him."

"Like that," I say. She nods.

I wrap my hand around hers, but she slides away, escapes.

Why won't you just love me, I ask her.

She says it's not possible to make someone feel something.

Even yourself, she says.

Even if you want to feel it.

I tell her about the life I have my eye on.

"Show it to me," she says.

We walk down to the store where I'd seen it, but it's no longer in the window.

Inside the shop I motion to the clerk, ask about the life I'd been hoping for.

"Someone bought it," he says. "Day before yesterday."

Kirthi looks down at her shoes, feeling my disappointment for me.

I'll find another one just like it, I tell her. A standard happiness package. Decent possibility. The chance of a kid. It wouldn't be enough for us, not quite, but we could share it, take turns living the life. One works while the other one lives, maybe I work weekdays and she gives me a break on weekends.

She looks at me for a few long seconds, seems to be thinking about it, living the whole life out in her head, then without saying anything, she touches my cheek. It's a start.

☐

When Deep was happy, before it got bad and then worse and then even worse, he was always talking about how he knew a guy who knew a guy who knew a guy. He talked like that, he really did. He loved telling stories.

About a week before he cracked up, we were in the coffee room and he told me a story about a guy at Managed Life Solutions, a mental-anguish shop across town, who made arrangements with a prominent banker who wanted to kill his wife. The banker was going to do it, he'd made up his mind, but he didn't want the guilt. Plus, he thought it might help with his alibi if he didn't have any memory.

Bullshit, I said. That would never work.

No, really, Deep says. He tells me all about it, how they arranged it all while talking in public, at work in fact, but they talked in code, etc.

Could never happen, I say. There are twenty reasons why that wouldn't work.

Why not, he said.

It's just too much, I said.

Too much what? There is no upper bound on cruelty, he said.

The next Monday, I came to work, and they were pulling Deep out the door, two paramedics, each one with an arm hooked under Deep, dragging him out, two security guards trailing behind. As they dragged him past me, I tried to make eye contact, but as he turned toward me I got a good look and I saw it: there was no one left. Deepak wasn't inside there anymore. He had gone somewhere else. He just kept saying, okay, so. Okay, so. Like a mantra. Like he was trying to convince himself. Okay. So.

And then the next day, there it was, in the newspaper. The whole story about the banker. Exactly how Deepak told it to me. There were rumors that he was the one the banker hired. He had been inside the body of a monster and the guilt had leaked through. Some things get through. People are not perfectly sealed. The technology of feeling transfer may progress, but something will always get through.

Or maybe not a monster. Maybe that's the point. Not a monster. Just an ordinary man, what a man is capable of.

Deep knew what was out there. There is no upper bound on sadness. There is no lower bound on decency. Deep saw it, he understood it, what was out there, and he let it seep in, and once it gets in, it gets all the way in, and it never comes out.

I open tickets. I do the work. I save up money.

Weeks go by. Kirthi opens up. Just a little.

She still refuses to look me in the eyes when we are kissing.

That's weird, she says. No one does that.

How am I supposed to know? I have not kissed many people. I have seen in American movies that people close their eyes, but I have also seen that sometimes one person or the other will sneak open an eye and take a peek at the other one. I think it makes sense. Otherwise, how would you know what the other person is feeling? That seems to me the only way to be sure, the only way to understand, through the look on her face, what she is feeling, to be able to feel what she feels for you. So we kiss, she with her eyes closed, me looking at her, trying to imagine what she is feeling. I hope she is feeling something.

I am at a funeral.

I am having a hernia.

I am having a hernia at a funeral.

I am in prison.

I'm at the dentist.

I'm at the prison dentist with a hernia.

I am in love.

I am in withdrawal.

I am in love with someone who doesn't love me back. I wish I had a hernia.

She takes me to see her father.

He has the look. I remember it. My own father looked this way.

He is living someone else's life. He's nothing more than a projection screen, a vessel, a unit of capacity for pain, like an external hard drive, a peripheral device for someone's convenience, a place to store frustration and guilt and unhappiness.

The thing hanging over us, the thing that's uncomfortable to talk about is that we could do it. We could get him out.

We stand there in silence for what seems like, for what is, way too long.

Finally, Kirthi can't take it.

He has only four years left on his mortgage, she tells me.

But, see, the way the market works, sellers like us, we never get full value on our time. It's like a pawnshop. You hock your pocket watch to put dinner on the table, you might get fifty bucks. Go get it a week later and you'll have to pay four times that to get it back.

Same principle here. I love Kirthi, I do. But I don't know if I could give sixteen years of my life to get her father out. I could do it if I knew she loved me, but I don't know it yet. I want to be a better man than this, I want to be more selfless. My life isn't so great as it is, but I just don't know if I could do it.

I am in surgery. For my hernia.

I am bleeding to death.

It doesn't hurt at all.

Things progress. We move in together. We avoid planning for the future. We hint at it. We talk around it.

I am being shot at.

I am being slapped in the face.

I go home.

I rest for a few hours.

I come back and do it again.

When I turned thirteen, my mother told me the story. She sat me down in the kitchen and explained.

"The day your father decided to sell his life," she said, "I wore my best dress, and he wore a suit. He combed his hair. He looked handsome. I remember he was so calm. You wore your only pair of long pants. We walked to the bank. You rode on his back."

"I remember that," I said.

"A man with excellent hair came out from some office in the back and sat down behind the desk."

I remember that, too, I told her.

You get, we got, forty thousand a year, she said.

My dad sold his life for a fixed annuity, indexed to inflation at three percent annually, and a seventy percent pension if he made it full term: forty years, age seventy, and he could stop, he could come back to us.

There were posters everywhere, my mother said, describing that day, the reunion day. The day when you've made it, you've done it, you're done.

There was a video screen showing a short film describing the benefits of mortgage, the glorious day of reunion. We would all drink lemonade in the hot summer air.

Just forty years, it said.

In the meantime, your family will be taken care of. You will have peace of mind.

"Time is money," the video said. "And money is time. Create value out of the most valuable asset you own."

*Don't miss out on a chance of a lifetime.*

When we went home, I remember, my father went to lie down. He slept for twelve hours, twice as long as normal, and in the morning, while I was still asleep, he rose from bed, washed and shaved his face, combed his hair. By the time I came down the stairs, he was just finishing up his breakfast, a piece of toast and a hard-boiled egg. I walked over to him and tried to hug him back, but I didn't have the strength. My arms were limp. So I just let him hug me, and then he went out the door and that was the last time I saw my father.

☐

Things stop progressing with Kirthi.

Things go backward.

And then, one day, whatever it is we had, it's gone. It won't come back. We both know it.

Whatever it is she let me have, she has taken it away.

Whatever it is when two people agree to briefly occupy the same space, agree to allow their lives to overlap in some small area, some temporary region of the world, a region they create through love or convenience, or for us, something even more meager, whatever that was, it has collapsed, it has closed. She has collapsed our shared space. She has closed herself to me.

A week after Kirthi moves out, her father passes away.

My shift manager will not let me off to go to the funeral. I live through funerals all day, every day. Funerals for strangers, crying for other people, that's more or less what I do for a living. And the one time I want to go to an actual funeral, the one time it would be for someone I care about, I'll be here, in this cubicle, staring at a screen.

Kirthi doesn't even ask if I would like to go anyway.

I should go.

I will be fired if I go.

But I don't have her anymore. If I leave, I won't have a job, either. I'll never get her back if I don't have a job. I'm never getting her back anyway.

I don't even know if I want her back.

But maybe this is why I don't have her, could never, would never have had her. Maybe the problem isn't that I don't have a life. Maybe the problem is that I don't want a life.

I go to work.

I open tickets.

I close tickets.

When I get home my apartment seems empty. It's always empty, but today, more empty. The emptiness is now empty.

I call her. I don't know what to say. I breathe into the phone.

I call her again. I leave a message. I know a guy in the billing department, I say. We could get some extra capacity, no one would know, find an open line. I could feel it for you. Your grief. I could bury your father for you.

Three days later, when I get to work, there is a note on my desk, giving the time of the funeral service. Just the time and, underneath it, she scrawled, okay.

Okay.

I arrange for the hour. At the time, I open the ticket.

I am expecting a funeral.

I am not at a funeral.

I can't tell exactly where I am, but I am far away. In a place I don't recognize. She has moved to a place where I will never find her. Probably where no one will ever find her. A new city. A new life.

She paid for this time herself. She wanted to let me in. For once. Just once. She must have used up everything she had saved. The money was supposed to be for her father but now, no need.

She is walking along a road. The sun devastates, the world is made of dust, but the day is alive, she feels alive, I feel alive for her.

She is looking at a picture we took, the only picture we took together, in a photo booth in the drugstore. Our faces are smashed together and in the picture she is not smiling, as usual, and I am smiling, a genuine smile, or so I have always thought about myself, but now, looking at myself through her eyes, I see that she sees my own smile starting to decompose, like when you say a word over and over again, so many times, over and over, and you begin to feel silly, but you keep saying it, and then after a short while, something happens and the word stops being a word and it resolves into its constituent sounds, and then all of a sudden what used to be a word is not a word at all, it is now the strangest thing you have ever heard.

I am inside of her head.

I am a nice person, she is thinking. I deserve more. She wants to believe it. If only she could see herself through my eyes. If only she could see herself through my eyes looking through her eyes. I deserve to be loved, she thinks. She doesn't believe it. If only I could believe it for her. I want to believe in her, believe inside of her. Believe hard enough inside of her that it somehow seeps through. She turns up the road and the hill gets steeper. The air gets hotter. I feel her weight, the gravity on her grieving body with every step, and then, right near the top of the hill, just the faintest hint of it. She is remembering us. The few happy moments we had. Okay, so. I am standing on a hill. I am looking at a color I have never seen before. Ocean. I am not at a funeral. I am thinking of someone I once loved. I don't know if I am her thinking of me, or if I am me thinking of her, her heart, my heart, aching, or its opposite, or if maybe, right at this moment, there is no difference. Okay, so. Okay, so. Okay.

# First Person Shooter

Janine is on line four.

"There's a finger in Housewares."

I don't ask what she means, because I can't think of anything funny to say, because I can never think of anything when I'm talking to Janine, because I'm in love with her.

I tell her I'll check it out and hang up the phone. The whole way over to Home and Bath, I'm just repeating to myself, under my breath, stupid stupid stupid stupid stupid dummy. The only thing that makes me feel better is that none of this really matters since I don't have a chance in hell with her anyway.

I hang a left at the towel racks and then a quick right and whoa, Janine was not kidding, that is definitely a finger. On the ground. In the middle of the aisle with all of the slow cookers.

This is the graveyard shift at WorldMart. Biggest store in the human world. I work Sunday through Wednesday, and then Friday if anyone calls in sick, which, of course, is pretty much every Friday. We're open twenty-four hours a day, three hundred sixty-five days a year, because keeping the fluorescent lights on for a decade or two until they burn out is actually cheaper than turning them on and off, and that means for eight hours every night there are two of us in here, minding the store, which is roughly the size of three city blocks.

I walk over to the nearest house phone and call Janine.

"We should tell Burt," I say. Burt is the manager. At the moment, Burt is not in the store. He's in the parking lot, a quarter mile away, listening to Black Sabbath with the windows rolled up in a smoke-filled Pontiac Sunbird. I can smell it from here.

"So tell him," Janine says, and there's something about the way she says it. It's a dare. She's daring me. It's a test. She's testing me. I start to wonder whether, despite all of the stupid things I have said to Janine, I might actually have a chance with her.

I hang up the phone and go back to where the finger is.

I pick it up.

Then I feel something cold and sharp tickling the back of my neck and I almost wet myself. A small yelp escapes from my throat.

I turn around to see Janine. I hate everything about her except for the fact that I love everything about her. I don't think I would actually ever want to kiss her so much as I'd want to possess her. Consume her. Eat her, so that no one else could have her.

"You should have seen your face," she says, laughing at me, but not quite mocking me. Not quite. Is this how she flirts?

I slip the finger into the pocket of my jacket. I don't know why, exactly, but I don't want her to see that I have it.

A bunch of stuff crashes to the floor over in another section.

"Sounds like Toiletries," I say, and we both run toward aisle ninety-seven. We stop in Mascara, crouch down, and listen to what sounds like shuffling. Janine starts crawling toward Lipstick and I try to grab her ankle but just end up with her shoe in my hand. She looks back, catches me watching her from behind, frowns, then motions for me to follow.

We stop at the Maybelline end cap just in time to see someone, or something, shambling toward a beef jerky sample station. Janine shrieks, and then the thing lets out a groan and then Janine and I are both up on our feet and running and we round the corner into Eyeliner and come face-to-face with it, whatever it is. Only, it's not an it. It's a her. A zombie. A woman. A zombie woman. She's older than Janine, closer to my age, maybe early thirties, missing a little bit of her face, but otherwise sort of pretty in a melancholy way.

"She looks nervous," I say to Janine, but Janine's gone, flat-out sprinting, screaming all the way to Power Tools.

Pretty Zombie Lady holds up two different tubes of lipstick, one bloodred and one that's more of an earth tone, and then I understand. She wants my opinion. I step back, look at her skin—which I guess is sort of a grayish baloney color—and point to the earth-toned tube.

"Matches your blouse better," I say.

She's holding the lipstick in her right hand, which has a hole where the ring finger should be.

I pull her digit out of my pocket and offer it to her.

She takes it and jams it into the hole where it used to be, and then sort of nods as if to say thanks.

She starts to creep over toward Accessories.

We shop for a while together like this. She picks out a couple of options, I give her my choice. Sometimes she goes with it, but a couple of times she goes the other way. At one point she stops in front of a mirror and looks at herself and I'm looking at her look at herself, wondering what is she thinking, and we lock eyes, we're making eye contact with each other in our reflections in the mirror. She's clearly thinking about someone. Me? No. This is crazy. But is it? I don't know. I don't know anything. I didn't even think zombies could think. And I'm thinking maybe she's not thinking, maybe she's under the control of someone else. Maybe I am, too.

Pretty Zombie Lady moves slow, and by the time she manages to pull together a decent-looking outfit, it's a quarter past two. Just as I realize that I haven't seen Janine in half an hour, I hear her voice booming over the PA system.

"I'm in Firearms," she says. "Stay low."

I pick up the nearest phone.

"She's not going to hurt us," I say, my own voice carrying out across the cavernous store. I just hope zombie girl understands me.

"What are you talking about?" Janine says. "She's going to eat us. She's going to eat our brains."

"No, I don't think so. That's not what she's doing here."

"Then what is she doing here?"

"Um," I say. "I think she's getting ready for a date."

Before Janine has time to process that, I look up and see Pretty Zombie Lady's face on the giant HD screen hanging over Home Entertainment.

"Huh," I say, watching her try to figure out the camcorder.

"What?"

"Gotta go."

Janine can hear in my voice that something's very wrong. "What's happening?" she says.

"Our friend just discovered *House of the Dead Two*."

I approach carefully, stop a few feet behind her. We both stand there watching the demo for a while, limbs being blown off, exploding heads, and when she turns around I see that, in her blank-eyed kind of way, she looks hurt. Betrayed.

Janine comes marching down the aisle with a hand cannon. Her skinny arm can barely keep it level. She's got it pointed at Pretty Zombie Lady, right at her head. The zombie just looks at Janine, unblinking, almost as if she wants to get her head blown off. Which, I suppose, is understandable. She started off tonight excited for a date, and then she comes in here and sees this game, and now who knows what's happened to her self-image, to her picture of the world. Is there such a thing as a self-aware zombie? Can a zombie realize what she is? Maybe there are degrees of zombification, and she's not quite all the way there yet. Maybe I'm partway there myself.

I put my hand on top of Janine's and slowly lower the

gun. Her hand is warm and full of blood and I should be excited to be touching Janine but instead I'm worried about Zombie Lady. She scratches her finger nervously until it falls off again and hits the ground. We all look down at it.

The *House of the Dead* demo is starting over. A bunch of zombie heads explode on-screen. Janine's still got the gun in her hand. I'm trying to figure out if this is the best day of work ever, or the worst. Why am I so self-conscious? What am I so scared of? It's now or never.

"Would you like to go see a movie on Thursday?"

"Are you asking me or her?" Janine says.

"Looks like she's already seeing someone," I say.

Janine looks at me for a long moment, like she's trying to look inside of me, almost as if she's noticing me for the first time.

"Yes," Janine says. "Yes I would."

I look at Zombie Lady, who is staring at us, slack-jawed. Whatever flicker of awareness I might have seen behind her eyes a moment ago isn't there anymore. She turns and drags herself toward the exit, and then, with a whoosh of the automatic double doors, she's gone.

"I wonder if she's still going on her date," I say.

"I'm pretty sure she's going to find Burt and chew on his brain," she says.

Janine and I stand and watch for what feels like a very long time, enjoying the mix of hot and cold air here at the boundary of the store, glad to be on the inside.

# Troubleshooting

**1**

It's a device. A device like any other. It takes in inputs and puts out outputs.

**2**

Acceptable inputs include: wishes, desires, thoughts, or ideas.

**3**

You have up to forty-eight characters, including spaces, so it's important to be honest with yourself. Punctuation counts, too.

**4**

Be careful of sentence fragments. Stay away from vagueness. Avoid ambiguity. Be clear. Be clear with your intentions.

5

It's like all technology: either not powerful enough or too powerful. It will never do exactly what you want it to do.

6

You are wondering: how does your desire get projected out into the world?

7

It is a kind of translation device. You translate the contents of your mind into words and then input them into the machine. The machine accepts those words and translates them into effects in the physical world.

8

When you ordered this thing, you thought you would use it for good. Everyone thinks that at first. It's harder than you thought it was. For one thing, what does it mean to do something for good? Do you know? Are you the best person to judge that?

9

Figure out what you want. Be honest. Put it into words.

10

Is language all about desire? Is desire all about loss?
Would we ever need to say anything if we never lost
anything? Is everything we ever say just another way to
express: I will lose this, I will lose all of this. I will lose
you?

11

Be specific. If you want an apple, will any apple do? Or
will only a certain apple do? That apple, there, right in
front of you, looking delicious. Is that what you want?

12

Is what you want to obtain a noun? Or is your objective
to verb an object? If you want to verb this object, how
would you like to verb this object?

13

There are objects you may desire but cannot explain.
There are objects that are not nouns, there are actions that
are not verbs. There are things we want that exist at the
edge of the forest, at the rim of the ocean, just over the
hill, just out of sight.

14

Beware of unintended consequences. Don't mess with
that button until you feel comfortable with the device,
its quirks and limitations. Cause and effect are tricky.
Don't like what's happening? Does it not seem correct?
Before you say it's not correct, here is a question: what is
correct? Correct assumes there is some universal registrar,
some recorder of your infinitesimal, momentary desires.
Correct assumes that there is some perfect mind, speaking
some ideal language, into some infallible translator. A
perfect three-way dictionary: mind to word to world.

15

You want sex.

16

You want to be a good person.

17

Imagine you are in a swimming pool.

18

You are lying on the surface of the pool, faceup, ears half
in and half out of the water. If you are doing this right,

you can hear the world below, the world above, and the inside of your head. You can hear all three worlds, the nether, the air, the boundary, like mountaintop radio stations, broadcasts cutting in and out, static, and secret, and fragments that sound like the truth.

## 19

Something is bumping into you from down below. What is it? Try to translate the subsonic whale moans, the floating, slippery intuitions into actual words, words spoken out into the dry half of the world. A self-translation, from your private underwater language. Bring it up, expose it to the oxygen and light. The unrefracted desire.

## 20

The problem with unintended consequences isn't with the consequences, it's with the unintended. Just because you didn't intend for something to happen doesn't mean you didn't want it to.

## 21

Place your thumbs on either side of the device and concentrate.

Hold steady.

Good.

Just a second more.

Thank you.


22

The following is a list of all of the momentary urges that
popped into your head in the last sixty seconds:

- You Know Who (at the office): one
  time, one afternoon, in your car maybe,
  or the unisex bathroom on 4
- Large orange soda in a Styrofoam cup, a little
  crushed ice, a straw, the kind with a bendy elbow
- Go for a swim (sounds nice)
- To remember the name of that one
  song, oh it's killing you
- To be two inches taller
- That new woman on 5
- A cigarette
- To quit smoking
- Head to stop pounding
- Hair to grow back
- Or at least stop receding
- That one who always wears that
  skirt, on 7 (in Marketing)
- A cigarette
- A hamburger
- No, a cheeseburger
- To be a better husband

- To be the world's greatest father
- A cheeseburger, then a cigarette
- To start over

## 23

Look again at what you said you wanted. Any vagueness or ambiguity in there? No? Is it possible the problem isn't that your words are vague? Is it possible that you are?

## 24

Let's be honest. What you really want to know is, how powerful is your will vis-à-vis the will of others with whom you come in contact? Others whose will may incidentally conflict with the effects you wish to bring about in the world. Others who seek to use their devices in order to directly oppose your will, as manifested in the world through your device. You want to know if you can make people do things against their will.

## 25

Here's the thing: that's not the point. The point is that it's a test. It's a test! Of course it's a test. You should not be surprised. The point is this: What does it say about you? What do you use it for? You know you should use it to help other people.

26

It will never do exactly what you want it to do.

You will never do exactly what it wants you to do.

27

This is what you have to ask yourself: Do you want to
be good, or just seem good? Do you want to be good
to yourself and others? Do you care about other people,
always, sometimes, never? Or only when convenient?
What kind of person do you want to be?

28

One more time, please. Place your thumbs on either side
of the device and concentrate:

- That new woman on 5
- A cigarette
- To start over again
- To go back to the first day of college
- To go back to the first day of high school
- That one trip to the lake, all four of you
- To be a decent person again
- To feel like a decent person
- To own a speedboat

29

You have been wanting all your life.

30
- To go nowhere in particular
- To go to Europe

31
You started as an infant.

32
You started life crying. Learned to talk so you could communicate your wants more effectively.

33
- To go to Alsace-Lorraine, wherever that is.
- (Page 138 in your eighth-grade French book.)

34
- Je vais à la plage
- Tu vas à la plage
- Il/elle/on va à la plage

35
You aren't going to get what you want. Not exactly. Not ever.

36

- Nous allons, vous allez, ils/elles vont à la plage
- Je voudrais aller à la plage, à la montagne, à la campagne, à la charcuterie. Je voudrais aller.

37

Even when you do get it, once you get it, you don't want it anymore.

38

- To be a better man
- To be a better husband
- To quit smoking
- A cigarette

39

You don't want this device. It will never do exactly what you want it to do. You will never do exactly what it wants you to do. You will never do exactly what you want *you* to do.

40

A life without unfulfilled desire is not what you want. A life without unfulfilled desire is a life without desire. The beach, you say. You want to go to the beach? Is that really what you want? The beach. The pool. The library. You want to go to the butcher, the baker, the supermarket. You want to go to the mountains and swim with friends in the lake. To want, in the infinitive form. To want, conjugated: I want, you want, he, she, one wants, we want, you all want, they want. Have you ever thought about not wanting, just for a second? Have you ever thought about putting a question into this device, about what would happen if you asked about the world, instead of just asking for it? Who do you think you are? Who do you think I am? What do you think you have in your hands? Why would you think you have any idea of what you want? You've had thirty-seven years to get it right, thirty-seven years with the device at your disposal, just waiting, ready, willing, and most nights you still go to bed confused, angry at yourself. When are you going to start considering the possibility that you are exactly who you want to be?

Please

## Hero Absorbs Major Damage

I could definitely use a whole chicken right now. But I keep it to myself. I don't want to alarm anyone in the group. They're all busy fighting demon dogs. These guys are literally killing themselves for what? Fifty points a dog is what. It breaks my heart. When I think of everything the group has been through together, the early days grinding it out in the coin farms, to where we are now, I get a little blue in the aura, I do.

I can still remember the morning I found Fjoork in that wooded area near the Portal of Start. He was just a teenager then, nothing on his back but a thin piece of leather armor, standing there like he'd been waiting since time immemorial. Like if I hadn't come along, he might have been waiting there forever.

I'll never forget what he said to me, there at the place where the road splits off into three paths.

One leading into the forest.

A second path across the great river and into the valley.

The third toward the north, up into the foothills and over the mountain pass, on the other side of which, as told in legend, lies the Eternal Coast of Pause.

And then Fjoork, all of three foot six, turns to me like he's known me all my life and says, without a hint of emotion

*Select Your Path.*
*I Shall Follow You.*

The "shall" is what got me. I still love it when Fjoork goes all shall on me. To have someone believe in me like that. I was what, twenty-two? And here was this sweet little guy all noble with his *I Shall Follow You,* as if I were someone, as if he *knew* I was destined for something good.

And now to see Fjoork like this, it just kills me, just makes me wish I'd made better choices, makes me wish I could take him to get an ice cream and wash off all that blood.

Trin and Byr are out in front of him, casting Small Area Fire over and over again. They aren't going to be able to keep that up for long, but they'll drain everything they have trying. That's how we are. We stuck together when everyone said we were all wrong for this quest, that we were a team built for flat-ground battles, that we'd never make it this far north, this close to the place without pixels.

☐

There were growing pains, for sure. We had to learn everyone's strengths and styles and weaknesses, had to learn to stop getting in the way of one another's semicircles of damage. More than once I got thwacked to the tune of

2d6 by someone's +1 Staff. There were days when it just seemed like the world was nothing but fields and fields of blue demon dogs, each one needing three stabs before it would disintegrate into a pile of sulfurous ash. So gross. Not to mention brutal on Trin's allergies. We learned and improved, and there was a point, not long ago, when it felt like we'd been through just about everything there was to go through.

And then word spread: an uncharted land to the west. An entirely new continent had opened up.

That's when things started to get bad.

Fjoork said, We Must Go! It Is Our Destiny!

Trin and Byr suggested marshaling resources.

Rostejn, being Rostejn, said to follow the action.

That made it two against two.

And I said, what are you all looking at?

Then my POV shifted.

And that's when I realized everyone was looking right at me.

As in: *We Shall Follow You.*

You. As in, me.

Me. As in, the Hero.

It all made sense after that. The odd feeling I'd always had, some kind of fixed radius around my position. If I moved left, the group moved left. Actually, if I moved left, the whole battlefield moved left. No matter what I did, I always seemed to find myself in the center of the action. Here. I am Here.

Because the center of the action was defined as: wherever I was. The way they were all looking at me, I didn't have the heart to tell them the truth. Maybe later, I thought, when the time is right.

So yeah, I led them in here.

I led a thief (Fjoork), two mages (Trin and Byr), and a swordsman (Rostejn) into a devastated wasteland: brutal terrain, limitless bad guys, and, as far as I can tell, pretty much no chicken.

Fjoork is still getting hammered on. Trin and Byr have run out of magic for at least two rounds and now each of them is just randomly stabbing with Ordinary Daggers.

Rostejn and I are the only ones who are doing any kind of real damage, but neither of us is feeling exactly Thor-like at the moment.

I'm not going to die or anything, feeling about thirty-five, maybe forty percent health. Rostejn looks like he's worse off than that.

We're finishing off a cluster of these hellhounds, hoping against hope we're close to a resting point, when a fresh wave of murderous dogs comes rushing in from the north. The worst part is their breath. Dog breath is one thing. And demons are generally pretty good about dental hygiene. But for some reason when you put the two together, it's like, oh boy, now, that's not fresh breath. Definitely not my favorite smell out here.

Rostejn's a couple of feet in front of me, and when the new batch shows up, I see his shoulders slump. He slashes a demon dog in the throat and cuts another one's legs off in two clean and efficient motions, then turns to look at me as if to say, chicken sure would be good right now.

I grunt in agreement.

Then it's just there. I don't know if it's the prayers to the deity that worked or we just lucked out, but there it is. A whole delicious chicken, cooked and on a platter, just sitting there under a tree.

Go for it, Rostejn says.

No you, I say.

Eat it, he says.

This is what it's all about. These guys, they all freaking love one another. And by guys, I am including Trin and Byr, who are like sisters, but also guys, but also, I might be slightly in love with Trin, like slightly and maybe also totally in love, like maybe ever since that double full moon in Oondar, when we spent a night flank to flank for warmth, but other than that, we are all like brothers, like chicken-sharing brothers.

Eat it, Rosti, I finally say, with authority. I tell him I feel great, only half lying. He needs it more, but even if he didn't, this is what a hero does, right? Right?

No really, right? I am really asking. I wish there were someone who could answer.

We set up camp for the night. Everyone is demoralized. Turns out that chicken Rostejn and I kept offering each other wasn't a chicken after all, just one of those smooth, chicken-looking-kind-of-rock mounds that stick out of the ground around these parts, so when Rostejn got nipped on the arm by one of those canine hell spawn, it took him down to twenty percent life bar and I'm sitting not so pretty myself at thirty-two, I just said to hell with it and used the Power Move I'd been saving for the last nine rounds. Lucky for everyone, it worked. But just barely. We all scrambled to this saving place, a little clearing near a cave. A place to hide out and heal our wounds, before setting out again in the morning.

We take stock of our equipment before dinner. A lot of it's pretty banged up. Byr has the whole mess laid out in front of her and Fjoork is reading off the scroll of items.

Shield of the righteous.

Check.

+1 short sword.

Check.

+1 long sword.

Check.

+1 medium sword.

Check.

+1 medium long sword.

Check.

"Jesus," someone mumbles.

"No wonder my back hurts," Trin says.

"Do we really need Blade of Slashing and Blade of Slicing?" Fjoork asks. Everyone knows it's directed at Rostejn. This is a thing with us. Too much baggage.

Darts of Severe Pain.

Check.

Darts of Moderate Pain.

Check.

Dagger of Nothing in Particular.

Check.

Chain mail's one thing, and everyone knows you can never really have enough Heal Wounds, or Elixir of Potency, but yeah, it's getting to the point where we need to make some changes.

Fjoork and Rostejn cook a meal together without saying a word. Afterward, we all pass around a wineskin and look up at the night sky.

Byr says, "Have you ever wanted to be something else?"

I want so bad to say yes. To tell them, I don't want to be the Hero.

"Probably a bard, I guess," Rostejn says. "I'm told I have a good singing voice."

"No," Byr says. "Not a different class. What if there were no classes? What if there were something, other than ranger or thief, paladin or mage? Something else. What if you could be anything?"

Fjoork says, "I'd change my name to something cool. Like Vengor, or Caldor. Or Steve. I mean, why do we all have to have weird names? Does that really help our quest?"

The fire burns down and the group drifts off to sleep.

I watch them all snoring, Trin the loudest. She's a single mother. Who is taking care of her kid at home? I don't even know. I am in love with her, and I don't even know who takes care of her kid.

Byr wakes up and catches me staring at Trin.

"She loves you, you know."

"Did she actually say that?" I ask her.

"Yeah," Byr says, throwing a stick into the fire. "But she thinks you'd be a shitty dad."

Eventually, I drift off into a restless sleep of my own. I dream the ancient dream, the immense dream of the ancients, I am looking out across the gray timeless expanse of Evermoor, having the greatest of all dreams, until just before dawn, when I wake to the sound of Rostejn relieving himself in the wooded area.

In the morning we set out for Argoq. Fjoork, who always seems to have a sense of these things, says he knows a guy who knows an elf who says to take the long way around, steering clear of the Lake of Sensual Pleasures. The group sort of grumbles, but everyone knows they have to stay focused on the mission, relentlessly scrolling toward the right.

We stop into a shop run by an old druid friend of Trin's. Trin greets him with a peck on the cheek. Seeing her kiss him slays me. I need to make a small saving throw just to avoid getting dizzy.

The druid shows off his new wares. Boots of speed, harp of discord, bag of merry diversion. The usual clatter thrown off by the steady flow of questers along the Silvan Route.

"How much," asks Trin, "for that Ring of Regeneration?"

"Fifty," the shopkeeper says, "but for you, twenty-five."

I fish coins out of my pouch and drop them in the keeper's hand. He gives me the ring, which I nonchalantly pass over to Trin, trying to be cool about it.

Byr raises her eyebrows at Fjoork, as in, hey, get a load of Grenner the Romantic over here.

Trin refuses it. "You need this a lot more than I do," she says.

I take it back, pretending not to care, and notice that Byr is suppressing a smile. OMG: how have I never realized this before? Byr is in love with Trin. She can barely contain herself.

I'm staring at Byr who is staring at Trin who is trying to pretend that this triangle of unrequited staring is not happening. Lucky for me, Rostejn breaks up the tension.

"Check this out," he says, holding up a vial of something yellow and bubbly.

"Oil of Reciprocated Feelings," the shopkeeper says.

"We'll take two," Rostejn says, flinging the coins onto the counter. I shoot him a look.

"What?" he says. "You never know when this might come in handy. You just never know."

□

It is a half moon later when Krugnor joins our group. We'd spent several days slashing through wave after wave of dumb meat, orcs and ogres. Toward the end, we were barely talking to one another, just carving up bodies, leaving them in piles. Green flesh hacked up everywhere.

Krugnor isn't any of the classic types. Krugnor is special, and everyone can see it right away.

It used to be there were only four kinds of people: fighters, mages, clerics, and thieves. What someone did for a living said something about who they were, what they thought of themselves, how they approached the world: strength, intelligence, wisdom, or charisma.

Krugnor, on the other hand, is part of the new generation.

"I'm a warrior-mystic," he says. That's how he introduces himself, when we find him by a babbling brook, doing yoga. "But I'm really not into labels. We're all just people, you know?"

I try to roll my eyes at Trin, but she's not looking at me. She likes him. I can tell right away. I look over at Byr, to see if she's noticing this, but even she seems to be in some kind of trance.

Even my own disciple is smitten. "We need that guy," Fjoork says.

So I put it to a vote.

Trin votes yes, tries to not look excited.

"He'll help with hit points," Byr says. "We could take on a thousand-ogre wave, if we had to. Brute-force our way through. Just plain outslug the monsters."

Rostejn votes yes, too, although I get the sense that he just wants to get at some of the hardware Krugnor is toting in his equipment sack.

And Fjoork looks head over heels for the new guy already.

No need for me to even weigh in.

Krugnor joins the group.

"Shall we make it official?" he asks.

I say, uh, sure, what does he have in mind?

"Stare into one another's souls, of course," he says. "Isn't that how you guys do it?"

I say, yeah, sure, okay.

Krugnor starts with Trin, big surprise, takes her head in his large, callused hands. They lock eyes and she seems to melt.

"So that's what a hero looks like," Byr says.

I tell Byr to shut up.

Each member of the group gets their own turn. When it comes to me, I take a pass, but Krugnor's not having any of it.

"If we are going to be brothers-in-arms," he says, "we will need to touch souls."

I tell him I'm getting over a cold.

"It was really a nasty bug. For your own good."

"Okay," he says. "But don't think you're off the hook."

After he's done with all the soul-staring, Krugnor asks me for a copy of the battle plan. I say, uh, yeah, I'll get that right to you.

It is foretold that there will be two hundred fifty-five battles in our path to destiny.

In the Final Battle, Battle 256, we will face the final boss.

Sounds pretty exciting.

And it was, for a while.

Today is Battle 253.

I think.

Hard to tell, though.

To be honest, epic battles of good and evil, they're pretty epic, but after about the first two hundred, they all start to kind of blur together.

☐

Before setting out to the battlefield, we pray to our god, Frëd. He's a minor deity, but sort of an up-and-comer. At least that's what he tells us.

We get a lot of shit from other groups for worshipping him, but he's really Byr's deity. Now that I think about it, she's partly responsible for this mess we're in. Before we became acolytes of Frëd, we all kind of did our own thing. And we definitely never talked about it, it was just sort of no one else's business who or what you worshipped or sacrificed poultry for, so long as you pulled your weight and your deity wasn't some imp who was going to screw with everyone or make us give up gold coins for safe passage or cause us to suffer ordeals. But then Byr went away to the north over summer vacation and when she came back she had that look like someone had cast Slightly Crazy on her, and she was all Frëd this, Frëd that, she couldn't stop talking about the guy, and we were all like, okay, cool, but you're not going to go all druid on us, are you?

"Frëd," Byr prays, "O Sort-of-Omnipotent One, protect

us today. Keep us safe, body and soul. Let us fight without fear, and vanquish our enemies."

"Or at least let us not get our asses kicked like last time," Rostejn adds.

"Goddammit, Rostejn," Byr says.

"No, no, fair enough," Fröd says, from wherever he is. We can't see him but his voice booms from on high. "I have to apologize for not doing such a great job the last few moons. I have gotten all of your prayers. Honestly, I've just been going through kind of a weird time."

Byr reassures Fröd. "You're fine. Seriously. You know we love you," she says, and everyone murmurs in agreement, but it's not the most reassuring thing to realize that the god you worship actually just wants you to believe in him.

□

Krugnor turns out to be an absolute beast on the battle-field. Not that anyone is surprised. He's ripped.

"Has to be at least Sixteen Strength," Rostejn says, watching him tear through some bad elves.

Byr's like, "Nuh uh. Seventeen, man. Easy."

Trin isn't even fighting, she's just standing there staring at the dude's muscles while he brandishes his +3 broadsword. I'm not even sure I could pick that thing up.

"Does he really have to fight with his shirt off?" I ask, but no one's listening. He flexes a lot, even when it doesn't seem necessary, and he can do that back-and-forth thing with his pecs. Ugh, look at him, just standing there in the river as it rushes by and splashes on his hardened body.

Even Fjoork gets in on the love fest.

"Did you see what he did to that kobold?" he says. "Split him clean in half, one-handed, with his short sword."

If I didn't know better, I'd think Krugnor had cast Infatuation on everyone. The guy is a totally cheeseball beefcake brooding sulking warrior type. Such a cliché. Although, I have to admit, I do feel safer with him out there in front.

Maybe that's what a hero looks like.

And for the first time since the quest began, I start to feel a little wobbly, as if my POV isn't so stable. As if the center of things is moving. As if the frame is unsure of who to follow, whose story it is. As if, maybe, I'm not so destined for my destiny after all.

We cross the highlands and come to a ridge, on the other side of which is the Valley of Aaaa.

"I've always wondered how that's pronounced," Rostejn says.

Byr says a prayer to Frëd as we begin our descent into the valley. We trudge through the Bog of Uncertainty. Trin reminds everyone to be careful of what we eat or even look at. Last time we were in the bog, Rostejn fell under the sphere of influence of a powerful mage in the Abjuration school and almost got everyone turned into black pudding.

Now we're in a dead zone for magic. Alteration prevails on one side, and Necromancy on the other. Neither one can practice in the other's region, as they are mutually forbidden schools. We walk the tightrope in between, maneuvering carefully, taking the narrow path, as shown on our scrolling map.

Krugnor follows my lead. Everyone else does, too. I try not to look too happy about it.

At one point we encounter some halflings, a quiet, intelligent people who live around these parts. One of their young has disappeared. The boy's mother is sobbing. Trin goes to comfort her. The mother explains that her son had fallen asleep on what he thought was a nice soft pile of leaves.

"Shambling mound," Byr says. The mother looks at us, unsure.

"A creature that looks like a heap of rotting vegetation," Byr explains. "But is actually a flesh eater."

"Yuck," Rostejn says. "That is nasty."

Byr shoots Rostejn a look like *real nice, idiot,* and the mother starts her crying again, even harder this time, and everyone is looking at me to do something, so without a word I leap straight into the mound, diving into the creature's body to grab the halfling kid, and then hacking my way out with a scythe. Which is messy, to say the least, and costs me about eight hit points, but in doing so, I level up. Everyone congratulates me, and I'm feeling pretty good. Even Trin looks impressed, and for a moment it doesn't seem so impossible that she might be in love with me after all.

The good feeling doesn't last long, though. The next battle is Battle 254 and we just aren't quite ready for this kind of onslaught yet, not tactically, not in terms of speed or weapons or as a team. Byr nearly dies, Rostejn nearly dies. Even my health dips down into the red zone.

I start to flicker in and out, a warning that my existence on this plane is in danger.

I know what I should do, but I can't bring myself to do it.

Another hit, direct to my torso, and that's it, my health is critical. My soul starts to tug itself out of its mortal coil, and my POV is floating up toward the clouds. I watch my body down there, fighting without spirit.

Frëd help us, I cry out, in a moment of desperation.

I can't see him, but I feel Frëd's presence next to me. "I thought you didn't believe in me," he says.

"Really? That's what you're going to say right now?" I say. "Seems sort of petty."

"Um, yeah," Frëd says. "Do you know anything about gods?"

He's got a point, I suppose, although really what I'm thinking is how come I've never noticed how high Frëd's voice is. I can't quite put my finger on it, but for the first time I realize there's something off about him.

"Byr's down there," I say. "She prays to you all the time."

"Yeah, but you're the one that's asking for help," he says. "Get on your knees."

"You can't be serious."

"For real, dude. I want you to pray to me."

So I start. "O Sort-of-Great One. O Exalted Mediocre One, Fröd."

"Get on your knees."

"You're pushing your luck."

Fröd uses some kind of POV shift power to direct my attention back down to the earthly battlefield, where my team is getting slaughtered. "I don't think you're in a position to be talking about luck right now."

I sort of get on one knee, like I'm going to ask him to marry me. Then I hear a woman's voice.

"Frëëëëëëëëëëëëëëëëëëëd," she yells. She sounds angry. Great, now there are two gods, one petty, one angry, and I'm still floating in the sky, getting farther from life with every passing moment. "You are in big trouble, mister."

Wait a minute. Is she? No. She can't be.

"Um, Fröd?" I say. "I think your mom's calling you."

"Not a word," he says. "To anyone."

"Sure, sure. Just kill those monsters for us."

"I, uh, I can't do that. Sort of used up all my juice for a while. But here's a chicken leg," he says, and disappears. "Sorry, gotta go."

I eat the food and gain just enough health to return to the plane of the living, where I see that Krugnor and Trin are in berserker rages and Rostejn has just used his Daily Power Move. The battle's pretty much over. The mini-boss, a frost giant, is on the ground, and one more thrusting attack by Krugnor does the trick.

Trin spots me reappearing and says, welcome back, nice of you to join us.

The mood at dinner is somber. No one's much inclined to be bawdy, or even merry. We chew on chicken in silence.

After dinner, I find Fjoork over by a stream, washing his face.

"Hey buddy," I say.

"Hey."

"Tell me again why you think I'm destined for greatness?"

Fjoork gazes off to the north, stands there just looking at nothing for a long time before answering.

"I never said that."

"You didn't?"

"No man. I said, I Shall Follow You."

"Oh," I say. "Yeah, you did. Huh."

Fjoork wipes his face, rubs the back of his neck.

"Well," he says. "This is awkward."

"Don't I feel a bit silly. All this time, I thought."

"Yeah, I know what you thought. And that's okay. It got us this far, didn't it?"

"I guess you're right."

"Who knows?" Fjoork says. "You might rise to the occasion."

And if not, maybe Krugnor will do it for me.

When I get back to the campfire, I see Trin and Krugnor sitting together on a fallen tree. Trin has her hands under her thighs, which she only does when she's feeling a little red in the aura. Now she's looking at him in a way I have never seen her look at anyone. She's definitely never looked at me that way, not even in Oondar.

Charisma's good for a few things. Bluff, Disguise, Handle Animals, Intimidate, Perform. But it's not so good when things get real. It's not so good heading into Battle 256 with a group of tired, beaten-down warriors. Right now, I'd trade half of my Charisma points for some Wisdom. I've always been a couple of points on the low side in that department. I think about gathering everyone around, to rally their spirits a bit. If only I could say something wise right now, or at least something wise sounding. Even that might not work. But I can't come up with anything decent, so I keep my mouth shut. Everyone's a little tired of me anyway, I think.

□

In the middle of the night, I wake up to Byr and Rostejn whispering in the darkness.

Krugnor knows where the map doesn't go.

Krugnor could lead us to The End.

We keep moving. We fight everything: deathknells, bugbears, carrion crawlers, lesser devils. We fight a small band of ghouls, and the ghoul queen. We get attacked by a gray ooze, waking up one morning to find the creature all over us, our camp, in our hair, covering our food. We lose almost an entire day cleaning up, not to mention using up several minor enchantments plus a Cure Light Wounds. We keep moving, to the right, slashing and stabbing, jumping and charging, dragging ourselves onward.

▢

Then Rostejn quits.

He comes to me and says, "You've been good to me, this has been good, but I gotta say, where is this all going? What are we doing? I don't know. I don't know anymore. I used to know. Now I don't."

"Ros," I say. "You are killing me. You are absolutely freaking killing me here."

How can I explain to him that I've been asking myself the same questions for the last ten moons? I can't say any of that. It will make me sound weak.

"Don't think this means I'm not grateful. Don't think this means, in any way whatsoever, that I don't appreciate everything."

"Yeah," I say.

"Yeah. Yeah, man. Yeah to all of it, all of our good times. You used to be such a great leader. We took down a gold dragon. A gold freaking dragon, man! We were the toast of the Forgotten Village. Free mead and game bird until we all got fat and out of shape and our Dexterity scores started going down and we had to quit that place and move on. You gave me my first blade. You taught me how to bludgeon. I won't forget any of that. It's just."

"I know."

"No, no, for real. There's something else," Rostejn says.

He cracks a smile, something I haven't seen for a long time. "I've got a girl now, boss. Met her right before we started this campaign. We've got a kid on the way. Gonna ask her to marry me."

"Wow, Rostejn," I say. "Wow. That's just, that's great."

"Yeah. I know. I know. Hopefully the kid'll take after his mother and be a peaceful law-abiding villager. Be more than I am. More than a sword for hire."

I tell him he's going to be a great father.

"I just don't know. I don't know what we stand for anymore. Byr's gone all churchy on us, Fjoork hasn't bathed in a moon and a half."

"That's not fair."

"It's not just you. It's all of us. Anyway, that's not the point. I've given up on the Path of the Immortal Hero. That's a young man's dream. I just want to get back to what I'm good at, basic stuff, level up every few years. Maybe go out and pick up a few skills along the way. I've always wanted to get into Animal Empathy."

"You?"

"Yeah, yeah," Rostejn says.

We have a warriors' embrace.

"If you're ever in the area," he says, "Jenny makes a mean boar pie."

"Sounds good," I say, sure that I'll never see him again.

□

Krugnor finds me as I'm walking back to camp and pulls me aside.

"There is something we should talk about," he says. "Man-to-man."

Here it comes. "Yeah, yeah. I know. Go for it."

"Go for it?" he says. He looks surprised that it was so easy.

"Yeah, be my guest."

Krugnor lunges forward and I am expecting him to knock me to the ground in some kind of display of alpha-male dominance, but instead he grabs the back of my head and shoves his tongue into my mouth. Way, way into my mouth.

It takes all of my strength to push him off me.

"What the hell was that, Krugnor?"

"You said go for it."

"That's what you thought I meant?"

"Wait, what did you mean?"

"I thought you were taking control of the group?"

"Why would I want to do that?"

"Um, I dunno, because look at you? You're this super-buff warrior-mystic who crushes evil and likes to aggressively shove your tongue down all of our souls? Because everyone thinks you are Frëd's gift to us?"

I hear some murmuring and that's when Krugnor and I both look over and see the whole group watching.

Trin's mouth is wide open. Rostejn looks actually sort of hurt, like if Krugnor was going to have a thing for one of the guys, it should have been him. Fjoork appears to be rapidly and violently recalibrating his view of everything that has happened for the last several weeks. Nobody speaks.

"Don't mind us," Byr finally says.

Krugnor turns back to me. "This is your group," he says. "Always has been."

"Then what the hell was with all of that flexing and showboating and stuff?"

"I was trying to impress you," he says. I look over at the group, and I can see it in all of their eyes. They're like, really? Trying to impress *him*? I know I've let them down, but it's not too late. If this new guy, this super-strong, super-charming new guy is willing to follow me, maybe they can find it in themselves to remember why they followed me in the first place. Maybe I can find it in myself to remember. Just maybe.

□

Or not.

It's the day of the final battle, Battle 256.

The first wave is lichs, and immediately we're in trouble.

Then the rocs start in from the sky. Byr is praying her ass off, but Fröd seems to be doing whatever gods do when they decide to ignore us down here, because about ten minutes into the fight I hear those dreaded words.

*Byr absorbs major damage.*

I do my Power Move, but it's a drop in the bucket. We're in a sea of enemy hit points here. A fresh wave of monsters comes over the top of the hill.

*Trin absorbs major damage.*

*Rostejn absorbs major damage.*

*Fjoork absorbs major damage.*

This couldn't get any worse.

Then it gets worse.

*Krugnor absorbs major damage.*

It isn't long before we are all exhausted, overwhelmed by the power and the sheer number of the enemy.

Then:

*Hero absorbs major damage.*

It can't be.

I am drifting off to The Place Where You Go Between Lives. I go through heaven, through hell, through an inter-dimensional nether region.

In the midst of the carnage, my soul lifts out of my corpse and toward a great expanse of light, the eternal horizon, the edge of the world, that final screen, how beautiful and peaceful it looks.

I have failed in my quest, and as surprised as I am that the story is ending this way, what is really unexpected is how okay I am with it, with all of it.

THE END

Really?
Is it really going to end like that?

I Am Here.

When I wake up in the sky, I am two hundred feet above the battlefield.

It is not pretty.

But on this side of The End, everything looks slow motion, almost like a choreographed dance, or perhaps a game, played by people that don't quite seem real anymore. Even my lifeless body down there looks like some kind of puppet, something to be pulled along, controlled and manipulated. The fighting goes on in silence, this gorgeous ballet of carnage, and I start to wonder, did it matter? Did any of it ever matter? I tried. I gave it my best. That's as much as anyone can say, right? So there. So that's that. And now, I find myself floating up to my eternal reward.

Then Frëd appears, sticking his big face through the clouds. I was right: he's a child. Hasn't hit puberty yet. A god-child. Even gods have to grow up, I guess.

"Hey Frëd," I say.

"Actually, no umlaut," he says. "It's just plain Fred."

"Well, good to finally meet you face-to-face, Fred."

"Things aren't looking too good for you," he says. "I'm sorry about all of this."

"Why are you sorry?"

He looks at me like, you don't know?

"What?" I say.

"This world, all of this, all of your world," he says, trying to find the words. The tingling gooseflesh of comprehension starts to creep up my arms and the back of my neck. My mind strains for a grasp of what it is he is getting at, like trying to visualize higher dimensions. Fred either can't say or doesn't want to say.

"I'm just sorry to have put you guys in this position," he says. "And now I have to go."

"So, that's it? That's all we get? No proper ending? The forces of good and evil, geography, history, destiny, when you have to go, you just pull the plug and all of this just goes away?"

"Let me ask you a question," Fred says. "What do you believe in? Do you believe in yourself? In your team? In heroism? In good? Do you believe in anything?"

"That was more than one question," I say. "I want to believe. I believe I am capable of believing."

"I guess that will have to do," Fred says, and with a wave of his hand the clouds part and projected onto the sky are two paths, two alternate futures for me.

In one direction is The Path of Legends:

*You have fought enough battles. Your record, while imperfect, is enough to earn you a place in the Hall of Eternity. Choose this path and you can vanish from the ordinary world. Perhaps you watch over the ongoing struggle, content in the knowledge that you have played your part. Perhaps you leave your plane of existence and become a minor deity yourself.*

In the other direction is Honorable Death:

*On the field of the most gruesome battle in history, you shall meet your foes and do battle. You may prevail. You may be defeated. You may prevail even as you are defeated. You may end up killing your enemy and, in the process, killing yourself. Rejoin your team now and find out.*

"Select Your Path," Frëd says, resuming his god voice.

Trin is bleeding from her eyes, nose, mouth, and ears.

Byr has lost an arm.

Rostejn has lost both arms.

Fjoork is in the process of being eaten by an orc.

Krugnor is looking up at the sky. He seems to have given up.

Maybe Frëd is just Fred. Maybe we have been praying to a nine-year-old whose mom keeps yelling at him to clean up his room. Maybe this is all just a game, an elaborate architecture created by some intelligent designer, out of what, boredom? Grace? Perverse curiosity? Some kind of controlled experiment or attempt to reconcile determinism and free will? What is my score? What is a health bar? Here I am, outside my own story, no longer moving to the right, or to the left. On the other side of the edge of the screen, off screen. After the end of the game, I can see it for what it was. You know what? I can know all that and still care. I can know all that and at the same time know that it matters. It has to matter. So our deity might have to leave for a while. So he may or may not have meant to make things this way. So we might be left on our own down there. So maybe he never meant for any of this to happen, this wasn't the story at all, he wishes he could just hit the button and start all over.

That doesn't make it any less real. That doesn't mean we should give up down here.

"I really gotta go," Fred says. "It's your story now."

He looks at me like, I'm sorry, but what am I supposed

to do? And he's right. He's a minor power at best. He can't get us out of this. He's a nice guy, good at what he's good at, but this is our problem.

I can see Trin and Krugnor down there getting their asses kicked. Things will suck if I go back down there. All of my friends might get killed. And even if they live, they will be horribly maimed and probably blame me forever for this shit that I got them into. But still. No one said it would be easy, or fun, or good, or clean, or that I would have any glory or comfort or a moment of rest in all of my days. But if I have anything at all I am still the Hero. I am here. This was my story. This is my problem. I'm going back down there to fix it.

# Human for Beginners

Living in close quarters with your Immediate Family you have no doubt begun to see the sometimes tricky dynamics, both fiscal and psychosexual, that often come into play between humans.

As a result, you may now find yourself looking around at other possibilities for joy, housing, points of reference, or shared sorrow. One rich and untapped source of experiential material is your Extended Family.

Extended Family Relations are often confusing for new humans, who cannot see the point of having human contacts that are neither potential sexual partners, nor business partners, nor enemies. The following may be useful in helping you sort through some of the many underutilized resources at your disposal.

### Cousins

Cousins are really the meat and potatoes of the Extended Family Relations menu. As the paradigmatic nonnuclear relative, they serve as the foundation of any well-diversified portfolio of human contacts. In a nutshell, cousins are your optional brothers and sisters. They are people to whom you owe nothing, who owe you nothing, but who can be important to you, if you wish.

## Aunts

Your aunt is moderately useful for experimentation, as a kind of laboratory for testing what will work and what will not work in your interactions with your human mother.

A word of caution: if you have a very oblivious-looking aunt, do not assume that she is what you perceive her to be, no matter how harmless she looks. Sensory data can be deceiving. Despite appearances, this aunt may be every bit as clever as your Earthling mother. In fact, she may very well be your Earthling mother, hiding in a different person.

There are other issues related to aunts that are beyond the scope of this volume.

## Cousins Revisited

Cousins can be a source of repeated use and considerable pleasure. This is especially true in your golden/declining years. As your genetically unrelated Persons of Life Significance (these are often called Friends or Enemies and will be covered in a future volume) begin to die away, or as you learn that you really know absolutely nothing about (and find yourself growing increasingly wary of) anyone who is not a blood relative, cousins can sometimes rise to prominence quite unexpectedly. Examples include: the Occasional Visiting Cousin, the Far Away but Close at Heart Cousin, and the very common General Proximity Cousin (who has moved to within fifty miles of your residence as one/both of you enter late middle age, for no good reason either of you can discern, other than the odd comfort of general proximity). Perhaps you have such a cousin. Perhaps you are such a cousin.

Great-Uncles

Great-uncles have been the source of much controversy in recent years. There are really two schools of thought on great-uncles. One school says that great-uncles are almost too tenuously connected to be of any relevance to you, being no more than a sibling of someone two generations removed. The other says that they love you very, very much. Both are correct.

Paternal Grandfather

Remember the simple rule: you are to your father as your father is to your grandfather.

Therefore, if you are male and terrified of your father, you should be exponentially more terrified of your grandfather.

There are other issues related to your Earthling grandfather that are beyond the scope of this volume.

## Cousins Part Three

If you have a great number of cousins, you may find it of interest to note the Mendelian ratios and allele distributions of certain physical characteristics among them. A chart can be helpful.

Note how dominant and recessive traits have distributed themselves among the second-generation offspring of your Earthling grandparents. Sometimes you will recognize that very similar subsets of the pool of genetic elements that make up your Earthling body can be recombined in subtly varying proportions to disastrous effect in your cousins. Or, you may find the opposite to be true. If either is the case, it may be hard to properly utilize your cousins.

Cousins often care about you more than you will ever know, or could ever possibly guess. It is not at all uncommon to realize this very late in life. To avoid the possibility of wasting potential affection, admiration, and shared sorrow, check to see if any of your cousins look up to you as an older-brother figure or someone whom they pattern their lives after, especially any only-children cousins you may have.

There are other issues related to cousins that are beyond the scope of this volume.

## Inventory

Every morning I find myself in a different universe.

There doesn't seem to be any order to the days.

One day I might wake up floating in the middle of a seething red ocean.

The next day I'm in a desert of frozen silver sand.

Most mornings, when I wake up, the rules have all changed.

Once in a while, though, I wake up in a place that feels comforting. The atmospheric pressure. The way gravity bends light, I can feel it: something familiar, something in my muscles, in my cells, my atoms.

First thing I do is tell myself who I am. This is right after I wake up, before I open my eyes. Who am I? Do I remember? Can I do it? Can I be honest? This isn't touchy-feely. If I'm not honest with myself in an empty, soundless universe, then who will be?

Second thing I do is I check for gravity. It's no fun crumpling to the floor or floating away.

I suppose the idea is this: I'm not real. I am some sort of alternate version of an actual person living somewhere in the actual world.

I have a Self. I'm his hypothetical. His guinea pig. His proxy, his personal test subject. I'm a lab rat in his thought experiments. A day player. The stunt double for his philosophical train tracks. A crash test dummy in a collision-testing facility for metaphysical safety.

It's not a comfortable realization, i.e., that I am, in fact, not a realization at all. But it makes sense. It explains a lot. Why I don't have feelings of my own. Why I always feel like I know what I was supposed to be feeling, but I can never just feel that feeling without being conscious of it, being aware of it.

Also, this feeling I've had, for as long as I can remember. A derivative feeling. I am not Charles Yu. I suppose that could be my name, too, but it has never sounded quite right to me anyway. Charlie, maybe. A secondhand version of the name. For a secondhand person.

The real me is out there, somewhere, sleeping soundly in his bed. Every morning, he wakes up the same person.

Every morning, I wake up some weird version of him.

Here is what I know about this Charles Yu person:

(1) He is a man.

(2) He works on the seventeenth floor of a downtown office building.

(3) He lives alone.

(4) He's lonely. But he hasn't always been.

Here's what I do not know about Charles Yu: pretty much everything else.

I do not know, for instance, how it is I come to enter a new universe. The mechanism for my entry into the world. I don't know how long I have lived like this. I don't know how, or whether it is even possible to predict what the world will look like the next day. I simply have to close my eyes, and wait until tomorrow in order to find out.

What is this condition? A permanent temporary. A
living and walking and breathing and thinking idea, an
almost-man. A contingency. Nothing essential to me,
nothing particular, nothing necessary. A sum total of
discrete moments, a long (or short) series of variations
on an underlying person, the sum of the area under
which might begin to approximate, in the aggregate, the
negative space of a man, all that he had not been, all that
he imagined he might have been, and so, in that sense, the
shape of me was the shape of Charles Yu, a Necker cube,
an etching by Escher, background and foreground, an "I"
limned by my real Self, my edge his edge, my boundary
his boundary, one line dividing a plane, a region of space,
one line creating two entities, the real and everything else.

Being what I am, I don't have direct access to the real world. I rely on inference. On what I see from moment to moment.

Charles Yu's world stays the same from day to day, hour to hour, while the world in which I exist changes whenever Charles feels like changing it. Or thinks about it. Or wonders about something. Or daydreams about nothing.

I always forget: am I the only one who knows that the world changes every day? Or do other people know, too?

Today I woke up as a man. My face is the same. Looks the same, anyway, as it did when I went to sleep. I'm looking at it in a mirror. I look okay. I feel. What do I feel? What is this I am feeling? I feel terrible. I feel like something just happened. Something big. What happened? Is that something the reason I feel terrible? If so, why do I feel terrible about it? Was it something I did, or something that was done to me? Or neither? Or both?

No one is in here with me. I'm in a room. A waiting area of some sort. Against the far wall is an aquarium with three fish: one striped silvery fish, darting in its movement, one goldfish, in the middle region of the tank, and a black fish, languid, fins trailing behind it like a flag. The water in the tank is seething, is red.

Are you waiting to see the doctor? someone asks me.

I didn't realize anyone was in here, I say.

You never do, she says.

Never? Really?

Never.

Wait, I say, do I know you?

No, she says. You don't know me. But I know you.

I get that a lot. People know me. I feel like I should
know them. I feel guilty that I don't. Like I should. I feel
superficial. I feel like I am a fraud. How can I not know
so many people who seem to know me? Is it possible to
go through life this way? Apparently, it is. I don't know
myself, I don't know my friends, I don't know the people
who populate my life. I can't be the only one. That
gives me some comfort. That's what I tell myself. I'm a
product of the world. A by-product. I didn't ask for this.
This thinning out of existence. This hollowing out. My
interactions with people are the bare minimum. I don't
feel anything. Ever. Hardly ever. Once in a long while. And
even then, it's random. The woman in the waiting room.
This receptionist. She knows me. Who is this person in
relation to me? How do I define our relationship, such as
it is? One-off, limited, formal, constrained, dictated by
our circumstances, whatever they are, dictated even by the
physical reality of the counter window between us, the
dimensions of the window. Is this someone I care about,
cared about? Or does she know the real me? That's it. She
knows Charles Yu. He's thinking about her. He's put her in
this room with me. Put us in here, with a fish tank. She's
about my age, dark glasses, a look on her face like she
knows the truth, a truth, about me that I should know, but
I don't. I think I feel something about her. I believe that. I
believe that I think I feel something. There's something.
That's a start. Except now she's gone. That was yesterday.
The day is done.

Why would anyone imagine themselves this way? Why does my Self do this to me? What is he waiting for? Who is he waiting to see?

What shapes can the world take?

A torus, a saddle, a Euclidean plane, on a brane, on a string, in a hologram, on a speeding train, in an infinite loop, a thirty-second universe, a maximal entropy universe, a backward-arrow-of-time universe. A no-causality universe.

On the worst days, I feel fine. On the best days, I know I am not.

Every morning I wake up knowing close to nothing. About myself. Or anything else. Every morning there is only one thing that can be counted on, one thing I can be sure of, without opening my eyes.

She is gone.

Who is she?

If I could just find some clue. I have a hard time even maintaining a thought, even holding an idea in my head for more than a few moments. I can't seem to build up any kind of momentum. Details distract me. I have a hard enough time just figuring out the rules each day. Putting them together, looking at them carefully, trying to discern a pattern, a progression, any kind of underlying meaning to it all, it just hardly seems possible. I'm the cargo, not the engine. My mind just goes along for the ride.

It's hard to have a relationship in this world. Other people are not the same from day to day. I might wake up next to a woman three days in a row, or three hundred, but I never know if she'll be there the next morning, or the next hour, or if the world will change completely while I'm not looking. She might even change into another person altogether. I might recognize something in her eyes, or she might not be a woman at all. She might turn into a man. Or a mailbox. Or a region of empty space. Or a feeling. Or a song. I might only recognize her as one recognizes someone in a dream, as in the way something is actually someone, and that someone is actually someone else.

This life: No need to bother with soul searching or trying to understand my nature or actions. No need to wonder why I am the way I am, why I do what I do. Just sit back and be whoever you are that day. I guess. I guess so.

Up. Morning.

I take an inventory of the world:

Me.

Check.

Bed.

Check.

Sun rising.

Check.

I wake up. It is late. She is gone.

What has Charles Yu done? What is Charles Yu trying to work through? Is that what this is? A laboratory, an experiment, a controlled space, a simulation, an iterative program to run again and again, under slightly different conditions?

I wake up. Take inventory. It's late. She's gone.

Underneath my life of random scenes underlies the script of his life, his worries and concerns and fantasies. Someday it will all make some sense. That's my plan, to keep plodding along, getting up every morning and going to bed every night, and in between, living through each minute, each situation, most of which make no sense, some of which are terrifying, if I keep talking to people, these people who seem both strange and familiar at the same time, if I just keep at it, that the real Charles Yu, my real Self, will emerge, what he wants or cares about or loves will make itself known.

It's late. She's gone. I take inventory.

A note.

From her:

*You don't know who I am.*

Also:

*You may never know.*

I have never seen her, let alone have any idea of who she might be. Does Charles Yu really know her? All he ever knew of her was who he saw every day. All I am is who I am every day. All anyone is to anyone is a series of days. Were they married? Were they in love?

How do I find her? How do I catch her? That's not how it works, is it? I can't control whether she's gone. She is gone. That's a given. There has to be a reason why she left. What am I allowed to do? What is possible? What is conceivable? Do all worlds have rules?

Do dreams?

Do they have gravity? Or physics? Chance? Or histories?
Do dreams have futures?

I wake up early. Or am I still dreaming?

The sun is rising. In the north. First sensation of the day: she's here. I go downstairs. That's her. Whoever she is. I look at her from the back, in a long shirt, her dark brown hair down just past her shoulders. I'm nervous. I don't know how long it's been since I've talked to her, I don't know if she'll remember me. What do I know about her? Let's see, she's young-looking. Younger than I would have thought. Wait, am I young? She must know I'm standing here. Name starts with. With an M? An M. That's good for now. Don't push it. It will come to you. Am I still in bed? I'm going to have to come up with a name if I'm going to talk to her. Or do I? If we're married, I wouldn't say her name. Not in the morning. Would I? Wouldn't I just kiss her, wrap my arm around her waist, nuzzle her neck? Is that what I'm going to do? What if that's weird? What if we're not like that? What if she hates her husband? What if we have a terrible marriage? What if, what if, what if? I'm trapped in a kind of what-if story, right? So what, big deal. Who isn't? Everyone I know is. What if you had quit that job, what if you had told him off, what if you had spoken up that one time, when it really mattered? What if you had made the choice you knew would have changed everything, would have made her and him and you all happy? What if the world ended today and you never told her you loved her? What if the world ended every single day of your life, and you still never told her?

What if Charles Yu hasn't lost anything? What if he is
perfectly happy? What if one day I could wake up as him,
flip it around? What if I could know what it was like to be
real? What if I found out that he had a wife and a child
and was genuinely happy? I imagine what that would be
like, to be happy, and to know that not everyone is, to
know that it comes at a price, and that price is a kind of
loss. The happiness and loss, intertwined, both of them
always existing at all times. What if I found out that the
real me was content, fulfilled, grateful? How could I be
happy for myself, while still remembering that someday
I will lose it all, everything important, and unimportant?
That everyone loses everything. Everything loses itself.
What if I found out that in my real life, my Self, this
Charles Yu person had never lost her, the woman? Why
would he do this to me? Why would he daydream about
the worst, the unimaginable? Why put me through that?
Is it for fun? To satisfy his curiosity? What if he needs
me? Needs me to complete him. One of us has something,
the other one loses it. Everything I have ever lost, I never
really had. I am the lost part of him, the lost side of him,
the part that never happened.

I wake up. I take an inventory. Here is what I know about Charles Yu:

(1) He is a man.

(2) He has a wife and a child.

(3) He is still happy.

(4) I will never understand him.

Things will make sense in the end. That's what I'm
hoping, anyway. Deep down, I've always felt that they
would, although lately I have started to wonder where I
got that idea, have started to wonder about what if. What
if I'm not doing this right? What if I missed something?
Slept through it, didn't notice, got distracted, just plain
missed it. For as long as I can remember, I have had this
before-feeling, this feeling like I am in the moment before
something is just about to happen, a feeling that whatever
is going to happen hasn't yet happened. Recently, though,
I have started to get another feeling. An after-feeling. My
whole life has been all before, before, before, leading up to.
And then, just like that, it feels like after. After-something.
Between before and after, there was supposed to be
something big, right? The present, the now, the moment.
What if I somehow skipped it, what if it passed me by and
I didn't recognize it, or worse, what if I never get to do it
at all? What if I go my whole life and never ask that one
key question, that one what-if that I am supposed to be
asking myself?

For a while, I thought I might be in a love story, but I hardly ever wake up next to anyone anymore. It still happens once in a while. When it does, the first thing I do, doesn't matter where I am, in the ocean, on the moon of some minor distant planet, doesn't matter where, doesn't matter if she knows who I am or if I know who she is or how strong gravity is or if I feel terrible or if the world is logically impossible, the first thing I do if she's there, is I tell her how nice it is to see her.

# Open

Samantha discovered it first. I don't know exactly how it started, just that I came home in the middle of the day and Samantha was standing there in front of the couch, and she actually jumped when I came through the door. I'm not sure why but that bothered me, maybe because I've always sort of suspected that people are only that jumpy when they have something to hide, and I was so much in my own head about being annoyed at Samantha that it took me a second to notice what she was looking at, which was a huge *word*, right in the center of the room.

"We need to talk about that," I said.

"Why? Why do we always have to talk everything to death?"

"The word 'door' is floating in the middle of our apartment. You don't think maybe this is something we need to discuss?"

□

We ate dinner in silence, pretending "door" wasn't literally hanging over us. Samantha went to bed early. I watched a show about poisonous lizards and drank warm terrible whiskey out of Samantha's coffee mug. After finishing, I put the mug back in the cupboard without washing it. When I slipped into bed I could tell by her breathing she was still awake.

"Say it," Samantha said.

"I'm not going to say it. You should."

"Why should I be the one to have to say it?"

"Because you brought that thing in there. That idea. You conjured it."

Our bedroom was tiny. I slipped my leg out from under the covers and opened the door with my foot, so that she had to look at it. But it was gone already.

"Samantha."

"I don't care," she said, with her back to me.

"It's gone."

"I told you to say it," she said. "Now we've lost our chance."

☐

I woke up at three in the morning to Samantha, with her hand under my shirt, running her fingernails up and down my back. She pulled in close and kissed the back of my ear.

"It's over," she said.

"I know."

"Do you want me to move out?"

"No, I'll find a place."

"Can you get me a glass of water from the kitchen?"

I went into the living room.

"Uh," I said. "You might want to come see this."

Instead of the word "door," there was now an actual door in the middle of our living room.

"This is like that movie," she said. "*Monsters, Inc.*"

"Actually it's like a poem I just read."

Samantha rolled her eyes at me.

"So are you going to open the door?" she said. I hesitated for a moment, and before I could say anything, she opened it and went right through. I stood there, too afraid to follow. Maybe a hole had opened up in the world, and movies and poems were coming through into reality. Or maybe we were the movie, or the poem, and this was our chance to go into the real world.

Just when I was about to go after her, Samantha came back through the door, giggling.

"Are you drunk?" I said.

"No. Okay, a little. Okay, a lot."

"You don't even drink."

She told me it was a dinner party. That everyone seemed to know her there. But it wasn't her they knew. Or at least it didn't feel that way.

"And there are all these other couples. And they know who you are, too, they keep asking about you."

"That's swinging. You're talking about us becoming swingers."

"Ew. Gross. No. It was not that at all."

"Then what kind of party was it?"

"People know us. They like us. Not 'us' exactly, it's hard to explain. You just have to come see for yourself."

□

It was us, but we were performing.

I could feel myself not quite being myself, but a little better, wittier, like I was doing everything for the benefit of someone else.

When I would talk to Samantha, it was like we were speaking lines. As if someone were watching, and we were trying to give off an impression. And the impression we were giving off was that we were happy, and in love, and that we flirted with each other and made each other laugh all the time.

At one point during the party, I put my hand on the small of Samantha's back, and whispered in her ear, "I love you," and it felt so natural that I felt like I really did, and it didn't matter that I never did things like that back on the other side of the door.

But it wasn't us. I had never put my hand on the small of her back. I didn't even like that phrase, "small of her back," and even as I was doing it, I felt more like I was "putting my hand on the small of her back" than actually doing it. It was a gesture more than an action, and I was not actually doing it because I wanted to touch Samantha. I was doing it just so that I could feel myself doing it, so other people could see that we were the kind of couple that showed each other affection in this way.

"I like it there," I said.

"We should go back tomorrow," Samantha said, and the way she said it, I knew she'd have gone back with or without me.

It was five a.m. We were in bed, lying on top of the covers, wide awake, our heads buzzing with the clinking of flatware and the hum of conversation.

We went back the next night, and the next. We were practicing something that we had no name for. Neither of us wanted to talk about what the "door" was. Neither of us wanted to take a chance that we might ruin a good thing. Every night, we would get home from work, get dressed without talking, and go through the "door." Whoever would get home first would call the other one to confirm that the "door" was still there.

We got good at whatever it was we were doing. We learned how to arrive at the party, and how to leave it. We learned to stay until just the right moment, the point in time during a party when you know you should make your exit, find the "door." If we stayed too long, there would come a point when the party had peaked, and everyone knew it, and yet there was nothing to be done. Being at a party at that point made everyone still there feel lonely, and trapped, and a little bit desperate. On the other hand, if we left too early, we would get home and feel like we'd left part of ourselves somewhere else, as if our centers of gravity had been displaced, moved somewhere in between Here and There, and we were no longer where we were. We were nowhere.

☐

I started to realize that I was more there than here. It was the same for Samantha.

When we had first started going through the "door," we lived our lives here, and went to the other side to be other people. But we were becoming those people, even though those people were us, and now, on this side, we were increasingly finding ourselves unsure of what to do, how to act or treat each other when there was no one to see how we "acted" or "treated each other." I would try to touch Samantha's cheek and she would move away. When she was getting dressed for work, I would try my old move, circle my arm around her waist, but she would turn around and give me a look, as in, what-do-you-think-you-are-doing. And even though I didn't show it, I felt the same way. It felt counterfeit, somehow, to be good to each other when it was just the two of us. It was as if. As if we were actors in a play with no audience, and I was still insisting that we stay in character, but she couldn't bring herself to do it anymore. Whoever we were on that other side had followed us through. We needed our audience to be us. To be "us."

I went less often, and eventually stopped going altogether. At first she said people were wondering what had happened to me, but after a while she stopped talking about it, and I didn't want to know. I assumed the story had changed. Or maybe she'd changed it.

□

One morning she came back from over "there" just as the sun was rising. She slipped into the bathroom to take a shower. I heard her singing a song I didn't recognize. She came out, dripping wet, drying her hair, still singing softly to herself.

"It doesn't make sense for you to keep your stuff here anymore," I said.

"I was thinking the same thing."

I went to go get her bag from the closet and that's when I noticed that the outer wall to our apartment was missing.

"Hey, you might want to come see this," I said.

She came out into the living room, still naked. We both stood there, as if being presented on a stage, standing on our marks, as if under an invisible proscenium.

"It's like we're in a diorama," she said.

I inched toward the edge and looked down. We were on the top floor of a five-story walk-up, and it was a good fifty or sixty feet down to the sidewalk. I could see the top of the large tree right outside the base of our building. I felt like this was an opportunity, or a sign.

It seemed like I should say something. So that's what I said.

"It seems like I should say something," I said.

"Look at that," Samantha said. She pointed to the word "open" hanging out there, just above the horizon line.

I thought back to that afternoon when we first saw the word in our apartment. How I had come home from work when I wasn't supposed to, when she wasn't expecting me, and how that disruption in our regular pattern had spread into a larger dislocation through the closed system of our physical and verbal environment. I'd come home a moment too early, before she'd had a chance to put her costume on, and something had changed, and we could never go back.

"There it is," she said, pointing to the place where our wall used to be.

And the word "door" was back, hanging there like an airship, waiting to take us somewhere. It started to drift away, and Samantha reached out and grabbed on to the first "o" and pulled herself up, straddling the letter, the quotes like wings, keeping her in midair. She looked at me, waiting to see what I would do. I wanted to ask her if she wanted me to follow her, but I knew that was exactly the kind of thing she couldn't stand about me. I could let her go by herself, and tell her I'd be here when she got back, knowing I would never see her again. Or I could go with her, and we could keep looking for new doors, we could keep going until we found the place, or the movie, or the poem, or the story. The story we were meant to be in together, the one where there were no more "she saids" or "she dids," the story where everything we said and did was exactly what we meant and felt, and if we never found it then we would keep opening doors until they were all open.

# Note to Self

Dear Alternate Self,

I read in the paper today about the quantum multiverse and how there are billions of me out there. Did you know about this? Anyway, I have a proposition for you to consider. If you would be interested in more information about my idea, please write me back and I will explain in greater detail what I am thinking.

Anxiously awaiting your response,
Me.
You.
Us?

||||||||||||||||||||||||||||||||||||||||||||||||||||||||||||||||||||||||||||||

Dear Self,

I was just about to write you the same thing.

Yours truly,
You

||||||||||||||||||||||||||||||||||||||||||||||||||||||||||||||||||||||||||||||

Dear Alternate Self,

You were? Whoa! Wait, what?

|||||||||||||||||||||||||||||||||||||||||||||||||||||||||||||||||||||||||||

Dear Self,

I think you're confused.

Yours truly,
You

|||||||||||||||||||||||||||||||||||||||||||||||||||||||||||||||||||||||||||

Dear Alternate Self,

I'm confused? I think you're confused.

Anyway, whatever. Here is why I'm writing. This morning, I was eating breakfast (I had Cheerios with thin slices of banana and nonfat milk), and I was reading the paper and came across an article in the science section about the multiverse (I don't normally read that section, but Cheerios with sliced banana is my favorite and I still had about a third of the banana left unsliced, so I had a second bowl, not a full bowl, about a third of the original bowl, so that the Cheerio-to-banana-slice-ratio would be correct). I had finished browsing the sports and business sections, and

|||||||||||||||||||||||||||||||||||||||||||||||||||||||||||||||||||||||||||

Dear Self,

You randomly picked up the Tuesday science section.

|||||||||||||||||||||||||||||||||||||||||||||||||||||||||||||||||||||||||||||||

Dear Alternate Self,

That's right. How did you

|||||||||||||||||||||||||||||||||||||||||||||||||||||||||||||||||||||||||||||||

Dear Self,

Know what you were going to say? Come on, dude.

|||||||||||||||||||||||||||||||||||||||||||||||||||||||||||||||||||||||||||||||

Dear Alternate Self,

Oh, right. Gotcha. Nice one, heh. Don't I feel silly.

|||||||||||||||||||||||||||||||||||||||||||||||||||||||||||||||||||||||||||||||

Dear Self,

I feel silly for you.

|||||||||||||||||||||||||||||||||||||||||||||||||||||||||||||||||||||||||||||||

Dear Alternate Self,

Anyway, what was I saying?

|||||||||||||||||||||||||||||||||||||||||||||||||||||||||||||||||||||||||||||||

Dear Self,

You were saying . . . wait, before we get into that, can I bring something up?

||||||||||||||||||||||||||||||||||||||||||||||||||||||||||||||||||||||||||||||||

Dear Alternate Self,

I think I know what you're going to say.

||||||||||||||||||||||||||||||||||||||||||||||||||||||||||||||||||||||||||||||||

Dear Self,

Yeah. You probably do. In fact, there's like a 99.99999999999 percent chance you do. You aren't my alternate self. You're still confused. Wait, does that mean I'm confused? Now I actually am confused.

First, and this is kind of a small thing, but it is not unrelated to the bigger thing that I want to say, there is the matter of how you address me. I don't think it should be "Dear Alternate Self." It should just be "Dear Self." I'm not a version of you, or a copy. I am you.

||||||||||||||||||||||||||||||||||||||||||||||||||||||||||||||||||||||||||||||||

Dear Alternate Self,

Identical in every way, down to the quantum state of every last particle. I couldn't agree more.

||||||||||||||||||||||||||||||||||||||||||||||||||||||||||||||||||||||||||||||||

Dear Self,

Right. And that's what this is about, isn't it? Quantum computation. That's why you are writing to me, to yourself, to ourselves. How can I be so certain? Because that's why I am writing to you. So don't call me Alternate Self. Just Self. You call me Self, I call you Self.

Dear Alternate Self,

Will do.

Dear Alternate Self,

Whoops, sorry.

Dear Self,

This isn't going to be—it can't be—a dialogue between the two of us, at least not in the way that you (and I) was/were thinking when we wrote that first letter to each other. You write to me, I think about what you wrote, I write back to you. Whatever interaction is to come of this, that's not how it works. Right?

Dear Self,

Right. Gotcha. On the same page now. Let's dispense with the formality of the letter and just write to ourselves, in one long letter. How does that sound? Sounds great. Good. Good. Good. Good. Good. Good. Can you stop that? Okay. Sorry. Sorry. Sorry. Stop it. Okay. Okay, so this is what we're thinking. You're getting us a little off track here, already, and for reasons that will become more clear to you, it's especially important for me to stay on track. The problem, I guess, is that I'm not exactly sure what that entails. That's why I am writing this to you. Actually, I don't know exactly why I am writing this to you. I just know that I am. Writing this to you, I mean. But wait, I guess I'm not even sure about that. First principles. Back to basics. Foundational assumptions. I am who I am. You are who you are.

Who am I? I am you. And you are me. Are we the same person? Depends on what you mean by person. I don't have a good working definition of person, which I am guessing means you don't, either. Assuming, as noted above, that in your reality there is still something called science fiction, you should be familiar with the idea of multiple universes. You have to be, because when I say "you" I mean my intended reader for this writing, which is, by definition, a version of me who understands this concept. Okay, so, multiple universes: the hypothetical set of multiple possible universes (including your universe) that together make up all physical reality.

Anyway, I guess this is probably the first thing we should have established.

The multiverse? It's real.

There are an inconceivably large number of copies of you. I'm one of them. (Are you sitting down? I am.) I'm not a particularly notable copy, I'm pretty sure there cannot be such a thing. But between you and me, I might be interesting, because, up until the moment you read the third sentence of this paragraph, you didn't realize that I existed, that there are countless versions of you and me out there. We had been trading letters back and forth, but we hadn't said it to ourselves, to each other yet. And now that we have, we both know it. You know it now, so I know it. And/or vice versa. I'm the one telling you this. I guess I'm notable in that I was sitting here, in my universe, and I realized that if there is a multiverse, then I should be able to communicate with other versions of myself by simply writing to myself in my own universe. The trick, I guess, the hard part, was in figuring out how to word it, and to whom to address it. I figured I had to couch it in terms that would be palatable to you, so I wanted to mention science fiction, but not actually call it that, so that you would know that I had a certain level of self-awareness, especially about how crazy all of this sounds. But now I am thinking that, since I could have called it science fiction, but didn't, there is a world out there in which I wrote this to you, but did call it science fiction, in which a version of you/me is reading this, thinking it is all science fiction, which is fine. Let's forget him—he was bound to happen anyway. He split off from us the moment we started this letter. You are my intended audience. And I suppose I am yours. So, I didn't call it science fiction, because, well, my life is real and so is yours and even though this may seem impossibly remote and fantastical and too abstract to matter, it matters to me, and I know that it matters to you, too, and sitting here, thinking about all of the possibilities, lost and never known, all of the regrets, all of the would haves and could haves and should haves, three different types of universes, all of them every bit as real as the one you are in right now. In fact, maybe you are in one of them. What is "is" to you is "could have" in the eyes of someone else.

What we've created here is a space, a kind of meeting place for other versions of ourselves. Like a time travelers' convention, it can take place anywhere. Just by putting this down on paper, by addressing a letter "Dear Self." My note to self is entangled with your note to self. So you're sitting there, like me, writing this to yourself.

We're corresponding.

We are correspondents corresponding in our corresponding universes.

Is that what writing is? A collaboration between selves across the multiverse? I've written stories that had to be wrung out, drop by drop, in the arid environment of the desert of your imagination.

You've written other stories that came in a rush, your forehead clammy, feverish, trying to just keep up with the words as they were pouring out—but from where? Nowhere you can go back to. Nowhere you understand. Do you think you know how writing works?

I've seen a lot of things, and you've probably seen a lot of things. What is happening right now as you read this? Am I the writer and you the reader? Or are you writing it and I'm reading it? If you think you are writing, do you feel like you know where it's coming from? If you think you are reading, is this information you are learning, passively? Or do you feel like you could be creating it? Does it occur to you as a voice in your head? Your own voice in your own head?

I feel, of course, that I am writing all of this, and it is all coming from me, but then again, how can I be sure?

How can I be any more sure than you are?

‖‖‖‖‖‖‖‖‖‖‖‖‖‖‖‖‖‖‖‖‖‖‖‖‖‖‖‖‖‖‖‖‖‖‖‖‖‖‖‖‖‖‖‖‖‖‖‖‖‖‖‖‖‖‖‖‖‖‖‖‖‖‖‖

*Dear Selves,*

*Hey guys!*

‖‖‖‖‖‖‖‖‖‖‖‖‖‖‖‖‖‖‖‖‖‖‖‖‖‖‖‖‖‖‖‖‖‖‖‖‖‖‖‖‖‖‖‖‖‖‖‖‖‖‖‖‖‖‖‖‖‖‖‖‖‖‖‖

Whoa.

‖‖‖‖‖‖‖‖‖‖‖‖‖‖‖‖‖‖‖‖‖‖‖‖‖‖‖‖‖‖‖‖‖‖‖‖‖‖‖‖‖‖‖‖‖‖‖‖‖‖‖‖‖‖‖‖‖‖‖‖‖‖‖‖

What was that?

‖‖‖‖‖‖‖‖‖‖‖‖‖‖‖‖‖‖‖‖‖‖‖‖‖‖‖‖‖‖‖‖‖‖‖‖‖‖‖‖‖‖‖‖‖‖‖‖‖‖‖‖‖‖‖‖‖‖‖‖‖‖‖‖

I don't know.

We split off again.

*You guys started without me!*

Aaaaaaghhh!!!

Don't flip out.
   Who are you, how did you get in here?

*What do you mean? I'm you. I'm totally you guys.*

No you're not. You're like, in a different font.

Aaaggh! What happened? What is happening?

I switched into his font!

**HEY GUYS**

Aaaggh! Now what's happening?

Okay, stop freaking out.

How can I not freak out? It's getting worse.

*Sorry I freaked you guys out.*

**I hereby convene the Hundred and First Annual Conference of Our Self.**

Who is that?

It's you.

No it's not.

It is.

I'm not talking anymore until I find out what's going on.

Me neither.

SAME HERE.

Hello?

**Hello?**

**Hello?**

||||||||||||||||||||||||||||||||||||||||||||||||||||||||||||||||||||||||||||

**Hello?**

||||||||||||||||||||||||||||||||||||||||||||||||||||||||||||||||||||||||||||

**Hello?**

||||||||||||||||||||||||||||||||||||||||||||||||||||||||||||||||||||||||||||

How many of us are there? *Hello.* Hello. HELLO. **Hi.** *Yo.*
We have a quorum. **Meeting's in session.** *Ready and
waiting.* Do we know what we're doing? What's the plan?
*Anyone have a plan?* **Anyone.** Someone go first. Please,
someone, anyone, go first. ***Someone, anyone.***

||||||||||||||||||||||||||||||||||||||||||||||||||||||||||||||||||||||||||||

☑ Thank You

# Yeoman

We reached the final frontier today.

Again.

No one wants to be the first to say it out loud, so it's one of those things where we have cake and beer and everyone mouth-smiles at each other while our eyes are all, does anyone even know what is going on anymore? As in, this is cool, for real it is, but seriously, what the hell.

I'm on the observation deck looking at it. The last world. Am I excited? Sure I am. Even if this is the seventeenth time we've been here. I'm excited. I guess we're still searching. Technically, I think we'll always be searching. As long as we are on this ship, have these uniforms on, we are searching. For something. Nothing wrong with that. But the thing is, to be honest, lately it has started to feel less like searching and a bit more like, I don't know, wandering.

Monday:

Monday mornings they announce the crew members for the week's away team, and it's always the same:

our captain, the XO, the medic, the security chief, the ethnographer, and an unnamed yeoman.

This week's yeoman: me.

Also: the yeoman always dies.

Information that would have been useful to know before I accepted the position.

They said, here is your new uniform.

They said, oh yeah, you get a pay raise.

They said, hey, how about a promotion? And I said, yes, yes, I've wanted to be a yeoman ever since I was a kid. To go down to the surface with the bridge officers. To wear that new uniform, get that little bit of extra money in the check.

They said, yes, yes, that's what it's like. They said, it's even cooler than you think. They said, great, great, good good, all good, congratulations.

No one said anything about dying.

□

Galactic HR assigns me a Coping Specialist.

We meet over breakfast in the nonofficers' mess.

He orders a Denver omelet, a bowl of cereal with two percent milk, an English muffin, grapefruit juice, coffee, and a Yoo-hoo.

"You shuh haf fomefing," he says, mouth full. He swallows a big lump of starch, washes it down with milk from his cereal bowl. "Breakfast is the most important meal of the day."

"How old are you?"

He says he's twelve, but if I had to put money on it he's ten, ten and a half, tops.

"Anything you want to talk to me about?" he says, stuffing a forkful of egg and bell pepper in his face.

"I'm good," I say.

"Fuit yourfelf," he says, chewing with mouth open again. A little piece of scrambled egg falls out.

I watch him eat way too much way too fast. When he's done, he wraps his English muffin in a napkin for later and hands me his card, tells me to call him if the whole meaningless-death thing starts to bum me out.

"Or if you start to experience fear-of-death symptoms," he says.

I ask him what a fear-of-death symptom might be.

He thinks about it for a second.

"Pretty much just fear," he tells me. "Also, extreme fear."

"Here's the thing," I start to say. I want to tell him that I'm married, that in less than three months I'll be a father, that dying this week would really throw a wrench into my family planning. I want to say all of it, but for some reason, I can't. So instead, I tell him he has a little piece of ham on his shirt.

"Score," he says, and pops it into his mouth.

Over dinner that night, I try to figure out how to explain it to my wife.

"They posted the list this morning."

"And?"

"You're looking at the newest member of the away team," I say.

"Yeah?" she says, reaching to take my hand.

"Yeah," I say, pulling my hand away.

"Wait, I thought this is what you wanted?"

"I'm the yeoman."

"Oh," she says. "Wait, what does that mean?"

"I'm probably going to die later this week."

"So, no movie night?"

"I am serious."

"So am I. I love movie night."

"I'm the yeoman," I say, raising my voice. "Do you know what that means?"

She shakes her head.

"The yeoman always dies."

She puts her fork down and doesn't say anything for a while, just sits there running her hand over the horizon of her pregnant belly.

"There's a small insurance policy," I say. "I got a packet from Human Resources, let me go get it."

When I come back into the room with the folder, she's putting on her coat.

"Um?" I say.

"This is bullshit. We are not living off a death benefit." This isn't how she talks usually, but then again, she's twenty-eight weeks pregnant. She is not messing around. "I'm going to see the captain."

"Whoa, whoa, whoa," I say. "You can't do that. You're not even wearing pants."

"You are not dying for this new job," she says, and she's right. It hurts to admit it. "I love you, but yeah, I said it. Your new job sucks. This sucks. Living in a converted closet sucks. You even kind of suck. The only thing that doesn't suck is this baby that we are going to have."

"You know, some people would be happy about this. It's a promotion."

She just looks at me like, who do you think you are talking to.

"Okay," I say. "I'll talk to him."

That night I lie awake, staring out into the cosmic background radiation, trying to figure out what I could possibly say to the captain that would make him think I'm worth saving.

Tuesday:

We're in the transporter bay. We beam down. Such a weird feeling. I wonder if anyone else is as excited as I am, but then I realize how dumb that is. Of course they aren't. They do this three times a week, and they're all bored of it. They're management. Comfortable. Lazy, really. Ever since they instituted free soft serve in the officers' dining quarters, the captain's Lycra has been looking a bit tight around the middle. It's hard not to notice.

As we're dematerializing, the captain starts in with the monologue.

You can tell when he's going to start with this

nonsense, because he sucks in his stomach a little. He always does this in the transporter because we're not allowed to move during molecular calibration.

And then he gets that off-into-infinity look. *It's the Age of Science Fiction,* he says. Everyone stares straight ahead.

*We have reached the point where our knowledge of the world now exceeds our ability to believe it, to believe what we are seeing, to believe what we are able to do.*

He has a way of speaking in italics.

*What we are capable of has caught up to, and even surpassed, our intuition about what should be possible. We have surpassed ourselves.* And even though I've heard this monologue five thousand times over the ship's speakers, and even though I know it was written by the ship's speechwriter, I can't help but feel just a little inspired, to remember just a little bit of what I felt, looking at the poster in the recruiting office that day, when I signed up for duty, imagining what it would be like to explore the universe.

And then we rematerialize on yet another world populated by sentient goo, and there's green glop everywhere, and it's oozing, which is how the glop procreates, and in the process of oozing, it makes a kind of groaning sound, and overall the whole planet smells like sulfur and even though it's hard, I try to remember that each and every place in the cosmos is an opportunity for discovery and that each and every life-form is a treasure and a marvel and a wonder, and I take out my Life-Form Analyzer so that we can catalog this wondrous, marvelous, slimy goop.

On the surface, we look to the captain for his plan.

"Meet back here in an hour?" he says, shrugging.

Everyone mumbles agreement and wanders off. The medic heads for the lip of a nearby crater formation, pretending to look at readings on his handheld. Security chief says he's going for a run. The XO is working on her résumé. She should have her own ship and everyone knows it. Instead, she's stuck as number two for the drunkest captain in the fleet.

The captain strolls off, practicing a new monologue he thought up in the shower this morning.

That leaves the new ethnographer and me. She doesn't look thrilled, but out of protocol introduces herself.

"Lieutenant Issa," she says, a little stiff. She holds her hand out like she's hoping I won't actually shake it so she doesn't have to touch me. She says she's going to head over to a nearby cave and see if she can learn anything about the mating process. "You can follow me if you want," she says.

I watch Issa collect slime samples for a while, with a very serious look on her face, but that gets boring so I wander over toward a nearby rock formation. There are weird noises coming from behind it. I look back at Issa to see if she hears it, too, but she's focused on her work, so I keep going toward the noise, edging around to behind the rock.

I hear what sounds like the captain, groaning. He's in trouble.

My muscle memory kicks in. I find a foothold in the boulder and hoist myself up onto the rock, just like we did in training. I land, ready to strike. I see the captain. He's down on the ground, shirtless, wrapped in some kind of slime, covering his face and mouth like a mask.

I jump down on top of him and with both hands and all my strength manage to wrench the slime off his face.

The captain jumps up. Actually, he sort of jumps up and back and off whatever he was crouching over, and now he's standing, flushed, with a wild look in his eyes and a fistful of goop in each hand.

"What the hell?" he screams at me.

I wasn't expecting thanks from the captain, no, but certainly not this.

That's when I notice that next to him is what appears to be a little sculpture that the captain has formed with his hands, out of goo. A little goo-person.

Oh.

The captain recovers his composure a bit, straightening out his uniform. "You didn't see anything, yeoman," he says, but not in a menacing, abuse-of-rank way. Even now, getting caught doing whatever it was he was doing, he's a little charming. Pervy, but still charming.

I guess that's why he's captain. "Let's keep this between us dudes," he says, and winks at me.

I say yes sir.

"It's just," he says, looking off into space. "It's not as easy as it looks. Wearing this uniform."

"Doesn't look easy at all, sir."

"Gets a little lonely out here," he says, and for a second I think he might be moving in to hug me. Instead, he reaches down and picks up a handful of goo and sort of fondles it in his palm. "You married, yeoman?"

"I am."

"Is she hot?"

"Sir?" I'm searching for an appropriate response, but he says never mind, so I turn and leave him alone with his goo-woman. Or maybe not alone. Who am I to judge? Maybe she brings him some comfort out here, out at the edge of this tired rerun of a galaxy.

Wednesday:

Another mission today. Another chance for random death. I don't think it'll happen just yet, still a little early in the week, but who knows? Yeomen have died on Wednesdays. Hell, yeomen have died on Mondays. We die. It's the job. It's actually in the job description.

### Duties and responsibilities, Yeoman, Second Class:
- assist in collection of soil and vegetation samples
- be prepared to die for no good reason

Not exactly a good job for someone with a kid on the way. I did a good job in Maintenance, fixed the quantum possibility engine so the officers could go off and mess around in alternate realities. And this is the reward. A promotion—to this?

We beam down and split up. I tag along with Issa again. She collects samples. I try to assist her.

"What are you doing?" she says.

"Trying to assist you?"

"Please stop."

"Look, I know you actually have a role to play. The thing is, I'm the yeoman, and I know you're kind of new as an officer, so I don't know if you know what being yeoman means in terms of my situation and all, but if you don't let me pretend to be helping you, I don't know what's going to happen to me."

Issa looks over at the XO, who seems to be sort of watching me, trying to figure out if I'm actually doing anything.

"All right," Issa says. "Pick that thing up and sort of wave it around in this general area." I tell her thanks.

We work for a while in silence, or rather, she works and I pretend to work, and it feels good, having a job to do, a purpose, even if it is a fake purpose.

It's late when we get back. We go through the ion-scrub and then debrief, and by the time I get back to my

quarters it's past two in the morning. My wife's in bed.
I slip off my uniform, slide under the thin blanket,
and drape my arm over her hip. She turns over and
faces me.

"Good God," I say. I don't know if it's the hormones or
what, but she seems to be literally glowing.

"Shut up," she says. "I'm huge."

"Yes, you are. And I like it."

"Did you talk to him yet?" she says.

 I don't say anything.

"You're just going to let this happen. To yourself. To us,
to your kid."

"What am I supposed to say?"

"How about, hey, Captain, I don't feel like dying for no
reason this week. You cool with that? Everyone cool with
that?"

"It's not like they want me to die," I say, but even as
I'm saying it, I'm remembering the slightly crazed look
I saw in the captain's eyes yesterday, playing with his
goo-woman, and I get a hollow feeling in the pit of my
stomach.

 My wife turns over and slides back into me. She takes
my hand and puts it under her shirt.

"That's not how this ends," she says. It's just this very
tiny, very pregnant lady, against the cold, dark expanse of
this who-gives-a-shit universe, and yet the way she says it,
it almost gives me a little bit of, I don't know, hope? As if
she could just refuse to live in a cosmos where that's how

this story could end. As if, by personal choice, by sheer will, she could collapse all of the possible worlds down to the one she wants, the one she needs.

Thursday:

Today's world is a wet one, filled with moisture-based life-forms. One breath of the atmosphere will cause you to know the answer to every question you have ever asked yourself. Where am I? Why did I do that? Was I right? Do they like me? Do I deserve love? Am I going to heaven? Why do I keep doing this? An answer for every question. All the answers, all at once. Not a pleasant fate, so we all put on our gas masks. No one really wants to know the whole truth.

And, of course, there's goo. The captain only seems to visit places with goo these days.

I wait all morning for a good moment, but the XO is still watching me so I have to pretend to be studying the environment. I make a face that I think of as Hmm This Life-Form Is Super-Interesting, and try to look as busy as I can.

☐

After lunch, I get my chance. Everyone is taking a smoke break, except for the security chief, who is doing yoga. The captain tells everyone he's going to take a leak and wanders off behind a grove of twenty-foot mushrooms. I wait a couple of minutes, then I follow him back there.

"Hey hey, look who it is," he says.

"Captain, I need to ask you something."

"Of course. Anything for my buddy. Assuming you've kept your mouth shut. Have you? Of course you have. Look at you," he says. "Okay, sorry, that was mean. What do you want, man? Make it quick. This goo isn't going to make love to itself."

I watch him play with the goopy substance, lovingly sculpting it into a sort of lumpy mound.

"It's Thursday."

"Yeah, so?"

"I'm the yeoman."

"Ah, yes," he says. He stops what he's doing and turns to look at me. "You want to know why you have to die."

"Yeah. Uh, yes. I mean, yes. Sir."

"Look, I'm not saying I'm happy about it. Or that I like it. I'm just saying, you know, it makes for a more interesting report. If stuff happens. As you can see," he says, gesturing toward his gooey girlfriend, "it's really freaking boring out here. And if Central Command ever realizes that, they'll cut my budget and I'll end up sitting behind a desk. So I need stuff to happen."

"I get that stuff has to happen," I say. "With all due respect, sir, I don't know if you know this, but my wife and I, we're expecting."

"Oh, boo hoo. What am I going to do, kill Issa? Have you seen her? She's super-hot. Kill my medic? Then how would I get my Vicodin, silly? You're the yeoman, dude. Do your job and die."

Friday:

No mission today, so in the morning I go down into Records. I find the quietest corner and ask the computer to pull up files on "Deaths, Weird."

Three hundred seventy-one weird deaths come up, and they're all yeomen.

Yeoman Tanaka died of laughter.

Yeoman Allen died of Leuchin fungus. According to the official report, it got a hold of her mind, and she wouldn't get back into the transporter area. As the ship pulled away, her mind was being eaten by the fungus, each of her memories being stored forever in a fat cell of the creature, to be replayed forever in an endless loop.

Yeoman Cooper died of fright. A forty-three-year-old man with advanced hand-to-hand combat training. Died of fright.

Yeoman Rhee died of thirst on XR-11uu7S, a water planet. Of thirst. Oh, also? She drowned. She died of thirst while drowning, which doesn't sound suspicious at all. The ship's log says the captain made a grab over the side of the raft, but sources close to the incident report that it "wasn't much of a grab."

I read for hours, into the evening, and they're all like that. Yeoman Nelson: indigestion. Yeoman Trammell: brain cramp. Yeoman Castellucci died from sneezing too hard.

Plausibly random-sounding deaths that the captain

could not have foreseen or prevented that, on further inspection, sound like exactly the kind of thing it would be cool to report in a captain's log.

□

I tell my wife about the records. She just looks out the porthole and doesn't say anything. We both understand what I have to do. I've got to find a way to avoid dying, but if I actually manage to do that, we don't know what would happen to her. She's got to get off the ship tonight.

We eat dinner in silence. I start to do the dishes but she says why bother. I help her pack a small suitcase. She's not mad at me anymore, she's way past that, but the fact that she's not crying is more than a little surprising. Sort of troubling.

Walking through the ship, we try to act casual, like we're on our way to the medical bay for an appointment. When we get to the right place, we look around briefly and then duck into the cramped area where trash is held before it gets ejected out into space. We find an empty shuttle pod and I help her in. I try to give her one final kiss but she just looks at me, so disappointed, and slaps my face gently.

"I'm not going to die, okay?" I say. "I'll find you somehow."

"I love you," she says. "But you're an idiot."

We hear someone coming and she shuts the hatch and I press the Eject button, and then she's gone.

Saturday:

It's a weird place to be. I'm not even mad about it anymore. I get it. This is my role. I get it.

We beam down safely onto the new planet and I breathe a little sigh of relief. At least it wasn't the transporter.

We do our usual thing, and by three thirty in the afternoon, the thought is starting to creep into my head. Maybe. Maybe I'm the one, the only yeoman to ever survive his whole week on the away team.

Around six fifteen, the captain gathers us up, gives us a little parable about what we learned here. The thought is definitely in my head now, but I don't even want to entertain it. More time goes by, and I'm thinking, here I am. I'm still here with fifteen minutes left.

It's eight minutes to seven when the captain says it.

"You," he says to me. Still doesn't know my name. I wonder if I even have a name.

"Captain," I say.

"I need your help collecting some samples," he says. "Over there."

Everyone tries to pretend they don't know what's happening, but as I'm walking away, I look back and catch them watching us, with grim looks on their faces.

We walk for a while. Far enough away so that, presumably, the rest of the team won't be able to hear whatever horrible thing is going to happen to me. "Over there, behind that huge space-thingy," the captain says. He actually calls it a space-thingy.

"You're like not even trying anymore," I say.

We go around the huge space-thingy and there, standing in front of us, is my wife, in all of her full-bellied glory, next to the shuttle pod I put her in yesterday.

"You, wha, how, uh?" I say. "You landed that thing?"

"Ugh, sometimes I can't believe I married you," she says. "The onboard computer, dummy. Hello? Technology? You don't even have to know how to do anything anymore to have your own ship." She looks at the captain. "Isn't that right, chubbs?"

The captain has a look in his eyes, half terrified, half in love with her, and I have to admit, she does look pretty incredible.

"What's going on here?" I say, and it starts to dawn on me. "Yesterday, when I was in Records, you."

"Went to see the captain, yeah. We struck a deal. I told him I'd prefer that my husband not die by himself on an empty planet," she says. "And he clearly doesn't want to be captain anymore."

"It's a win-win," the captain says, getting into the trash pod. "Your wife's a smart woman."

"What are we going to tell the crew?" I say.

"Trust me. The crew is not going to care."

Then my wife pantomimes killing the captain, pretending to smash a rock against his head while he makes elaborate and overly detailed dying sounds, both of them smiling at each other the whole time, like a couple of kids pretending to be space explorers.

Sunday (and Beyond):

In the end, the official report listed the cause of the captain's demise as "Death by Space-Thingy." An inquiry was made by Internal Affairs at Central Command, but that was quickly wrapped up when it became clear that all the crew members' stories were consistent. *Yeah, man, the space-thingy just totally came up and got him.* The captain got to live out the rest of his years alone, on that planet, humping a pile of alien goop or whatever it is he wanted to do. The ship's officers voted to give my wife a commendation, which she gladly accepted, and a job offer, which she politely declined. We had a party to celebrate our new captain (the former XO) and as usual there was cake and beer but it was different because, for the first time in a long time, we felt like we were searching again. In her first official action as our new captain, she admitted that we were totally lost, which everyone knew but the previous captain had been unwilling to admit, and she said that our new destination was home, wherever that might be, and we all agreed that it was as mysterious and noble a pursuit as any, and we all set our sights that way, hoping it would still be there if and when we found it.

# Designer Emotion 67

PharmaLife, Inc.*
Annual Report to Shareholders
Fiscal year ended May 31, 2050

Our solid work in Depression has led to increasing market share in Dread. It is a step in the right direction, and although I know some of you may have doubts, I believe that we can collectively rise to the challenge. Hello, my name is Tripp Hauser. For those of you who weren't able to make it to the continental breakfast meet-and-greet this morning, allow me to introduce myself: I am your humble chairman and chief executive officer of PharmaLife.

I've been with the company for thirty-four years, and I started, like many employees, in Hair and Erection or, as everyone called it back then, baldness and boners. I worked my way up from the mailroom, an eighteen-month tour

---

* PharmaLife, Inc., is a corporation formed under the laws of the State of Mississippi, a territory of the United States of China, and a wholly owned subsidiary of The Acme Widget Company of Ohio.

of duty, and then there were the obligatory rotations in Sleep, Allergies, and Fat, with a quick stint in Cholesterol. I'm proud to have spent my entire career here at Pharma-Life, and also proud to announce the results of our recently ended fiscal year. But as interesting as I am, you aren't here to listen to me talk about myself. You want to hear about it.

*It.*

*The whispers. The rumors.*

*Number 67.*

We'll get to that, but first we have to talk about some other boring stuff, like money. So much money. So, so much. It's crazy how much profit we make! It's almost criminal. Okay, my lawyer Cutler is giving me a dirty look. Sorry, sorry, legal-man. Cutler is such a tight-ass. I love him, though. Love you, Cutler. All right, let's dive into the numbers.

As disclosed in our publicly available filings with the SEC, our Depression group launched a new product, Zyphraxo-zol☺™, in Q3 of 2049, and I am thrilled to report that positioning of Zyphraxozol☺™ is pretty much kicking our competitors in the shorts. The new slogan, Be the Person You Wish You Were™, has tested high in all four quadrants. I personally oversaw the refinement process as a team of researchers succeeded in reducing incidence of side effects by a statistically meaningful amount versus placebo, while increasing average patient-rated euphoria/despair axis values from the mid- to high 70s to the low 80s. Now, to those not versed in the lingo of the industry, this may not strike you as a huge improvement, but in a hypercompetitive field with a mature product, where the J&Js and the Eli Lillys and the Bristol-Myers Squibbs of the world are killing one another on the broadcast airwaves and in the courtrooms of the Federal Circuit and in the mindshare battlefields, killing one another over tenths of a point, a move from 78.6 to 81.2 in a single product upgrade generation is unheard of. Please trust me on this. Unworldly. The stuff that careers are made of. If I weren't already CEO, I'd promote myself. (I could be my own boss! Wait a minute. Can I do that? Is that possible?)

[Txt msg to Cutler: pls chk w/HR dept.]

Where was I? Yes. Depression. Depression has been good to us. But at this point, as you all realize, it has come to be run as an exercise in sales and marketing. We're late in the product life cycle. The Depression-industrial complex has been built. Winning in the Depression/Suicide space these days means keeping the machine running smoothly. With each new generation of the product, we crank up the engine a little: spreading the early word at physician conferences, getting the collateral out there, pens and squeeze toys and magnets and little foam footballs, legitimatization (i.e., commissioning the articles in *JAMA* and the *New England Journal of Medicine*), and then postlaunch, from the sourcing of raw materials all the way to fill and finish, to keeping the distribution channels stuffed full, bursting with product, to the shelves of the pharmacy, to the medicine cabinet and nightstand, to the mouth, stomach, liver, bloodstream, brain, mind, and life/day/worldview of the end user, lifting off her soul the heavy wool blanket of melancholia. But you don't care about that. This is what you care about: bottom line. Which is this: Depression earned three forty-two a share last year, or just over nine and a half billion dollars for PharmaLife. Not depressing at all!

[Take a drink of water. Smile at someone. Mean it.]

Moving on to Advanced R and D (the official name being the Division of Research and Engineering on consolidated Anxieties (social, general, low-grade existential) and Despair, or DREAD). Depression may have matured and become a marketing shop, but the DREAD business unit is still the domain of the engineers, a basic and applied science shop, still at the exciting phase of its life cycle, on the upslope of the knowledge curve, and everything is up for discussion. It's an exciting time over at DREAD. Come to the Millbrae campus and ask for a tour of the DREAD wing. It's just an intellectually stimulating place to be right now. The other day, I walked into a VP's office and what do I find? Books. An executive with books in the office. He was even reading one! Right there in the office. During the workday. He had reference materials on any of twenty different subjects, ranging from still-to-be-published papers from some quantum computing wonk at the Bell Labs, to doctoral theses, to "secret" files from counterparts at competitors, all the way down to undergraduate primers on cognitive science, neuroscience, evolutionary psychology, probability. We are not messing around, folks. We are going to cure dread by the end of the decade. And by cure, I mean, find a blockbuster drug that has a differential rate of indication greater than the margin of error in white mice that exhibit symptoms of dread. Or whatever the mouse version of dread is.

[Txt msg to Cutler: pls Google "what is it like to be a mouse."]

Our researchers have. We're going Phase II, then Phase III, and then the FDA approval, all in eighteen to thirty months. And then we're going to get this out to doctors, we're going pump humans full of this stuff, just flush that dread right out. Dread will be a thing of the past.

Okay, the next part, I'm going to read this part really fast, and I encourage you not to listen carefully because it's just stuff that the FDA is making me say: users in the trial have reported a number of side effects, including, for instance, slight madness, moderate madness, jitterbug leg, jitterbug legs, jitterbug foot, zombie foot, zombie toe, acute slappiness, chronic slappiness, and the crazies.

Also, dry throat, dizziness, diarrhea. All minor side effects.

Confusion. Meh.

Disorientation. Big deal.

Vertigo. Whatever.

Also may cause: liver spots, vision spots, partial vision loss, total vision loss, more-than-total vision loss, bruised kidney, itchy kidney, itchy foot, itch-in-a-place-that-is-inside-your-head-that-you-can't-reach, random arterial swelling, random arterial bursting, loss of consciousness, splitting of consciousness, loss of mind, partial zombi-fication.

But come on, people. Would you rather be confused and disoriented with a dry throat and the runs, or would you rather feel dread? I don't even have to ask.

Look at that ticker today. Our shares are up thirty-one

percent year to date. Eight percent just while I've been talking! [Txt msg to Cutler: SELL SHRS NOW. HA HA J/K. BAD FOR PR! DUH. BUT SRSLY, SELL SOME IF U CAN.]

All right, friends, let me now address the rumors that something big is going on behind the doors of Building 43. Yes, yes, everyone's heard the rumors. Those rumors are not true. Except for the ones that are true. I disclaim any connection to those rumors, except for the rumors that I personally started. Nothing big is going on in 43. Because big doesn't even begin to describe it! It's unimaginable. Industry shaking. And you know I'm not one for over-statement. So let me just say: the northeast corner of the tenth floor of Building 43 is working on something that the world has never even imagined. Designer Emotion 67. What is it? That's what you all want to know. You are sitting on the edge of your seats. That guy right there in the front row actually just fell off his seat. You okay, Chief? Vertigo? Diarrhea? Been taking too many of our products? Kidding, kidding. VP of Sales hates my guts now. There have been murmurings in various conference rooms and enclaves and kitchen nooks around campus. There are leading theories. A psychoactive drink that allows for instant Nirvana (thirst-quenching Zen in a plastic easygrip bottle). That's not it, although we do have interesting new products in the Buddhism-Taoism experiential consumer product space. Some say it's a sense-enhancer that works together with memory so that you can have a picnic lunch that you will never forget. Because you literally will not be able to forget it. Your first Little League home run. Your first kiss. If you live to be a hundred and ten, the experience will seem as intense as the day it happened. Relive it anytime you want, anywhere. Just don't accidentally have a bad day when you take it! The memory will haunt you forever. We are working on this product. But that's not it either. I can confirm that. What I can't confirm is what's going on in 43. I'm just not going to say one way or another what it is. Or maybe I will!

[Clear throat authoritatively.]

At this point I should probably address some of the ugly insinuendo that has been floating around. What? What did I say? That's not a word? I am quite sure it is. Can I keep going? Thank you. At this point, the insinuendo has gotten to the point where it has been weighing on the stock price, which affects me a lot more than most if not all of you, ha ha, so I should care even more than you do. And I do. Let me just begin by stating unequivocally a few things that are untrue. I mean, the statements I am referring to. That's what's untrue. Not what I am saying. I am saying the truth. I am going to be truthfully referring to some untrue statements. You know what I mean. Number one: we are not laying off a million and a half employees next month. Absolutely not true. That is a round number. Very round. There is no way the number will be exactly 1.5 million people. That would be crazy. But kind of cool, you have to admit. Okay, now the VP of Human Resources is giving me major stink-eye. Okay, sorry, sorry. Let me get back on track.

[Compassionate tone:] You have been hurt. Some of you, maybe, since in addition to shareholders, there are employees in this room with stock awards from your employee savings plan. You think you have been hurt as employees by some of the policy changes, and that an apology is in order. I hear you and this is my response.

[Clear throat with humility.]

I hereby apologize on behalf of the company for your hurting; provided, however, that it is expressly agreed by all of you that such apology shall in no event be construed as an admission of guilt, blameworthiness, culpability, involvement, intention, recklessness, negligence, fraud, error, omission, regret, sympathy, empathy, or acknowledgment that you have been harmed. To all of you who may be hurt in the future, or have been hurt in the past, or are hurting now, or all of the above, due to anything that the company has nonnegligently not done, I do not apologize because it's not PharmaLife's fault, but I do acknowledge your hurting, and may I humbly suggest that you consider purchasing some of PharmaLife's products, maybe even some of you worked on these products! We have a diversified line of products dealing with pain of all types, and it is my offer to you to buy them, at full price, which is win-win, as it benefits you, and the company in which you hold shares. Cutler! You are ruining this. Cutler, our company lawyer, Cutler is laughing, ladies and gentlemen, because I was joking. We do have it. The rumors are true. Emotion 67. It's a pill. It's the pill. The meaning pill. God pill. Is that what the kids are calling it? It does what you think it does. We're the industry leader in pharmaconarrative products, and we're going to make a killing. You are all going to be very rich. Thanks for your time, and your continued investment in PharmaLife. Thank you for believing in us. Thank you for believing in our ability to deliver belief. Questions? Kidding, Cutler, kidding. Sorry, folks. No questions allowed.

# The Book of Categories

**0**   **What there is**

**1**   **Proper name**
  The full name for The Book of Categories* is as
  follows:

THE BOOK OF CATEGORIES
(A CATALOG OF CATALOGS
 (BEING ITSELF A VOLUME ENCLOSING
A CONCEPTUAL STRUCTURE
 (SUCH STRUCTURE BEING
COMMONLY REFERRED TO AS AN
 (IDEA)-CAGE)))

**2**   **Nature of**

  **2.1**   **Basic properties of**
    The Book of Categories is composed of two
    books, one placed inside the other.

---

* Which itself is listed in The Book of Books of Categories, Volume
III, p. 21573, Row K, Column FF.

The outer book (formally known as "The Outer Book") is a kind of frame wrapped around the inner book, which is known as, uh, The Inner Book.

### 2.1.1 Paper

The Inner Book's pages are made of a highly unusual type of paper, which is made of a substance known as (A)CTE, so called because of its (apocrypha)-chemical-thermo-ephemeral properties, the underlying chemistry of which is not well understood, but the practical significance of which is a peculiar characteristic: with the proper instrument, (A)CTE can be sliced and resliced again, page-wise, an indefinite number of times.

#### 2.1.1.1 Method for creation of new pages

Each cut must be swift and precise, and the angle must be metaphysically exact, but if the operation is performed correctly, there is no known lower bound to the possible thinness of a single sheet of (A)CTE paper.

### 2.1.1.1.1 Page count

To wit, as of the time of this writing, despite having total thickness (in a closed position) of just over two inches, the Book of Categories contains no less than 3,739,164 pages.*

## 3 Intended Purpose

### 3.1 Conjecture

This property of repeated divisibility is believed to be necessary for The Book of Categories to function in its intended purpose (the "Intended Purpose").†

### 3.2 Theories regarding Intended Purpose

There are four major theories on what the Intended Purpose is. The first three are unknown. The fourth theory is known, but is wrong.

The fifth theory of the Intended Purpose (the "Fifth Theory") is not yet a theory, it's still more of a conjecture, but it has a lot of things

---

* And counting.
† The Intended Purpose is unknown, so this is basically just a wild-assed guess.

going for it and everyone's really pulling for the Fifth Theory and thinks it's well on its way to theory-hood.

### 3.2.1 Unsubstantiated assertion (status: in dispute)

Whatever the Intended Purpose may be, this much is clear: the book is a system, method, and space for a comprehensive categorization of all objects, categories of objects, categories of categories of objects, etc.

## 4 What there is not

## 5 Mode of propagation

### 5.1 How the book changes hands

On the left-facing inside cover of The Framing Book, we find the word "DEDICATED," and underneath, two lines labeled

"From: _____"

and

"To: _____."

### 5.2 Each possessor of the book

attempts to impose her numbered ordering of the world by adding categories.

**5.3** **At some point, whether out of frustration or a sense of completion, or a desire to impose such system on others,**

a possessor will pass the book on to another user, by excising his or her name from the To line, placing the name in the From line, and then writing in the name of the next possessor of the book in the To line. The excision should be performed with the same instrument used to cut new pages.

**6** **As you may have realized**

**6.1** **What this means is**

The Book of Categories contains what is, in essence, its own chain of title. It is a system of world ordering that has, encoded into itself, a history of its own revision and is, in that sense, the opposite of a palimpsest. Nothing is ever overwritten in The Book of Categories, only interspersed, interlineated, or, to be more precise, inter*paginated.*

**10** **A man named Chang Hsueh-liang**

has possessed the book seventy-three times. No other individual has owned it more than six times.

**7** **Why**

7.1  Why
would someone ever give this book away?

8  A man

8.1  Looking for what was there

8.1.1 Trying to name it

8.1.1.1 Naming being one way
to locate something not quite lost,
and not quite found

8.1.1.1.1 A name also seeming
to be a necessary AND
sufficient condition to
possession of an idea, a name
being a kind of idea-cage.

10.1  Little is known about Chang, a general in the
Chinese army, except that he is believed to
have lost a child, a newborn daughter, in a
freak accident while on a brief holiday with
his family.

9  Something else you need to realize about the book

9.1  Is that
The sheer number of pages in the book is such

that ordinary human fingers cannot turn the pages in a reliably repeatable fashion. Simply breathing in the same room as the book will cause the book's pages to flail about wildly. Even the Brownian motion of particles has been known to move several hundred pages at a time.

9.2 **If you ever lose your place in the book**
it is unlikely that you will ever be able to return to the same page again in your lifetime.

[INSERTION—START]

**6.1.1 One reason**
why someone would give this book away: at some point, whether out of frustration or a sense of completion, or a desire to impose such a system on others, a possessor will pass the book on to another user, by excising his or her name from the To: line on the

[INSERTION—END]

**5.2.1 Each possessor of the book**
The various possessors of the book can be traced, from which*

* Thackery T. Lambshead himself has been the caretaker of the book

### 10.1.1 The incident

Onlookers who witnessed the incident
say there were no words in their language
to describe what occurred, only that
"the water took her" and that although
"nothing impossible happened," it was,
statistically speaking, a "once-in-a-
universe event."

## 10.2 It is unclear whether Chang

was repeatedly seeking out the book, or it kept
finding its way back to him.

## 10.3 A medal of some sort, and two insects,

are believed to have been placed inside the
book by Chang.

### 10.3.1 The general problem of categorization

Although it is worth noting that the
location of these objects is unstable, due
to a phenomenon particular to The
Book of Categories known as "wobbling,"
which can result from stored conceptual
potential energy escaping through the
frame of The Inner Book and resonating
with The Outer Book.

---

on two separate occasions, each time receiving it from Bertrand Russell, and each time passing it to Alfred North Whitehead.

**10.5  It is clear from certain sites in the book**
that Chang remained obsessed with naming
what had happened to his child.

**10.5.1 Chang's last entry**
is a clump of (A)CTE paper consisting
of hundreds of thousands, maybe
millions of blank pages, known as The
Chang Region. On each page of The
Chang Region of the book is written
what appears to be an ancient form of a
Chinese character. Scholars disagree as to
the identity of the character.

**11    Eventually, a possessor of the book comes to
realize**
how hard it is to find any given page, lost among the
pages. Trying to find that slice, to cut through it on
either side, before the page has been lost.

**8.1.1.1.1.1 A name actually being**
a memorial to the site where an
idea once rested, momentarily,
before moving on.

**8.1.1.1.1.1.1 If you listen
carefully,**
you can hear it in there, but
when you look inside, the

idea-cage is always empty,
and in its place, the concrete,
the particular, something
formerly alive, now dead and
smashed.

### 10.1.1.1 Chang's daughter

was five weeks old when she died.
For reasons unknown, she had yet
to be named.

# Adult Contemporary

Murray chooses The Brad™ and right away feels he's made a mistake.

"Let me ask you something," the sales guy says. "Do you feel you're making a mistake?"

*It's like he's in my head,* Murray thinks, but he tries not to show any indication either way because this guy's good and he knows it, and Murray knows it, and the guy knows Murray knows it. The sales guy's name is Rick, which strikes Murray as an appropriately false name for an unusually false person. Rick says something rehearsed about how you should try to do at least one thing each and every day that scares the living crap out of you, or some similar scrap of wisdom from a daily inspirational calendar. The truth is, though, that Murray does want to be scared or, if not exactly scared, then perhaps just a little out of control, or a lot out of control, that feeling of not knowing what is going to happen next but also, on top of that, or maybe underneath that, or wrapped all around it, a feeling that the danger is temporary and all part of a larger scheme, toward his ultimate triumph or redemption or at least escape to safety. His whole life Murray has always felt like something was just about to happen, but never quite seems to, as if any moment now, his life is about to start, the day is approaching, when all of it starts to come together or fall apart for the purpose of later coming back together, the feeling that every little detail, from the coffee he spilled on his shirt this morning to the song he heard on the radio in his car on the way here, the time he spends staring in his bathroom mirror wondering what is so unlovable about his face, Murray wants to feel that all of it, all of *this* is lead-ing toward something big, wants to feel anything, as long as it is real.

The sales guy puts the paper in front of him and shows him where to sign and Murray is confused: *this is a real estate contract?* The sales guy looks like he has gotten this question a million times and smiles a smile that Murray thinks is probably meant to communicate, *hey, nothing to worry about, you're in good hands here,* or something like that, but the gesture, a kind of practiced sincerity, is having the opposite effect.

"It's a 2BR/2BA lifestyle," Rick says.

"It's a condo."

"We prefer to call it a managed experiential product," Rick says.

It's warm in the room, and Murray has been sitting here, his complimentary iced lime-passion-fruit green tea sweating onto the salesman's desk, for close to an hour, going back and forth between The Brad™ and The Jake™. How the heck is he supposed to make a choice like this? Just like this? Right here and now, locking himself in forever? *No, no,* the sales guy reassures him, Murray has seven days to change his mind, no questions asked. In fact, *it's actually state law,* Rick says, as if he had just remembered it, but it sounds to Murray like just one more part of the pitch, like a line, as if Rick is just reciting from a script, verbatim, right out of a playbook, right down to the word "actually," which Murray realizes should make him feel icky, like a customer, but actually the *actually,* the idea that there might be a script, that this sales guy whose real name may or may not be Rick, the possibility that this Rick or "Rick" sitting across from him might not really be talking to Murray but in some sense performing, that is *actually* what finally gets Murray, not so much the performance by Rick (or maybe the performance by "Rick") itself but what that would imply, the prospect of a structured interaction, of *going through something,* what Murray has always thought of as the stuff of life, the chance that, for once, he might get to be tangled in that stuff, a bit of drama for an old guy like Murray who all his life has never really been able to afford much in the way of drama. What does he have to look back on, to look forward to? He is retired now, after forty years, with a small pension, small but enough. A widower, with a few friends, and a son who doesn't call him enough. *Maybe I am making a mistake,* Murray thinks, *but maybe that's what's been missing.* Mistakes. Risk. The chance of something going right. The willingness to look like a fool in the hope that he might actually get to feel something again.

So Murray signs.

Rick congratulates him on his decision, and right

away the air-conditioning kicks in. Murray feels a little bit tricked, realizing they'd been keeping it warm all that time, but before he can think too hard, Rick is moving Murray along.

"What is that?" Murray says.

"That's your sound track," Rick tells him.

"Who picked it?"

"It comes with The Brad."

"Does it seem kind of loud to you?" Murray asks.

"You'll get used to it," Rick says. "People can get used to anything."

Murray has a hard time believing it. "Seems kind of loud."

"Come on," Rick says. "Let me show you to your new life."

Then he flicks open a hidden compartment on the side of the desk and touches a button and the walls fall away. They're still sitting at the desk but now the desk is outside, they are outside, in the middle of a very large, very dark green lawn, the grass mown immaculately, smelling so much like grass that Murray almost wonders if what he is smelling is actual grass or a laboratory-synthesized version of the odor of grass that smells even more like grass than grass itself.

"What's your favorite season?" Rick asks Murray.

"I don't know," Murray says. "Fall, I guess."

Rick hits another button and all of the leaves on the trees begin to float down from the branches, great flat blankets, canopies of yellow and orange and ocher and now the air smells different.

"I've always loved Autumn®," Rick explains. "It has the best music."

Murray can smell a mixture of things: the wafting perfumed air that hits you when you walk into a fancy department store. A little bit of that new car smell. The smell of paper and high-quality ink from a mailbox full of glossy brochures, catalogs for expensive home appliances. A leafy, windy smell. The smell of cold itself, the smell of wanting to be indoors, shaking off your coat, the smell of the season of roasting things and sipping things and buying things.

"The Brad is our most popular offering in Adult Contemporary," Rick says. Murray looks down and realizes they are on some kind of path indicated by a painted golden line, subtly blended into the landscaping, but clearly demarcating their course. Rick pulls a gleaming key from his pocket and hands it to Murray with a bit of a flourish. Murray puts the key into the keyhole and turns it. With a heavy click of the tumblers, the faux-mahogany door opens and they are both hit by a wave of new-house smell, the chemical-tinged perfume of clean carpets, a swirled-together mixture, aromas of wood and leather and fresh paint.

Murray stands there inside his new The Brad™ taking it all in. On a flat-screen television in his entryway there is a listing of today's lifestyle events.

"There's tai chi by the duck pond at two thirty today,"

Murray says, reading from the schedule. "Followed by an ice cream social on the lanai."

"Yes, yes, there is that. And so much more," Rick says. He tells Murray that it's a series of emotional flavors, designer moods, a Palazzo-level recreational narrative.

"Timeshare," Murray mumbles. "You sold me a time-share."

"Yeah," Rick admits, breaking character. "I did, didn't I?" Rick allows himself a slight grin, a little internal high-five for another sales job well done.

"I still have seven days to change my mind."

"This is true," Rick says. "But you won't."

"How do you know?"

Rick takes a deep breath, closes his eyes, and is silent for a long five seconds. Then he puts his hands firmly but warmly on Murray's shoulders and looks him in the eye.

"Murray, I have to tell you something. You made a huge mistake. You should have trusted your gut instinct."

"What?" Murray says, with more than a hint of panic. "What are you talking about?"

"You have cancer, Murray," Rick says with a heavy, insincere sigh. "I'm so sorry."

"I don't understand," Murray says. "How could I have cancer?"

Rick hands Murray a nine-by-twelve manila envelope. Murray's name and Social Security number are printed on a label in the upper right-hand corner. Murray takes it, and it feels stiff and surprisingly weighty, as if there might be a thick sheaf of lab results in there, or X-rays, or some other grim document laying out his future as a set of probabilities or regions of fuzzy dark gray, darkness and grayness that are growing by the day.

"Wait a minute, did I have cancer before I bought The Brad? I don't understand. Did you give me cancer?" Rick gives him a look that is both patronizing and beneficent, as if to say, *don't be silly,* and also *I care about you, you silly old fool, don't you know how much we all care about you?*

"You wanted something to happen, right?" Rick says. "For all of this to be leading up to something? Closure," Rick says, pointing at the manila envelope. "That is definitely one way to have closure."

"I didn't say I wanted closure. Drama. I said I wanted drama."

"What do you think drama is, Murray?"

"How about something more open-ended?"

"Oh sure, that can be arranged, too," Rick says. "But even open-ended stories have to end at some point, right? Open endings, after all, are still endings."

Then Murray realizes that he never said anything about drama. He thought about it *in his head.*

"What, just because it's in italics you think I can't hear it?" Rick says. "That was part of your story, too. Your inner monologue. All of it. It's all part of Murray Choosing The Brad."

*Who are you?* Murray thinks. *Or what are you?*

You haven't figured it out, yet? I'm your narrator, Murray.

You're a sales guy.

Sales guy for a narrative experiential lifestyle product, narrator. Just titles, really. My job is to sell this story to you. To make it yours. To make you believe. To make you feel something again. Isn't that what you wanted?

The Brad™ they are in disappears, roof, then ceiling, then the walls one at a time, then the floor, then the furniture, each layer and element dematerializing in sequence, and then Murray and Rick are standing in an empty city, Vancouver shot for Los Angeles, Toronto shot for New York, night shot for day, not eternal yet somehow hourless, a place yet somehow unplaceable, an architecture trying to be everywhere and in doing so becoming nowhere.

"Where is this?" Murray asks.

"It's a commercial break."

Murray notices that all of the cars are luxury sedans, white and featureless. With a burst of accompanying indie rock, a silver coupe comes slicing around the corner, tight suspension and race-car handling and tinted windows, and the whole world goes into slow motion, all of the other cars and all of the other drivers, except for the hero car and its driver, who has a smile of perfect self-satisfaction, and Murray realizes this is his chance to make a break for it, to escape Rick and The Brad™, and Murray, no spring chicken really in the winter of his days, nevertheless takes off running down the alley and sees a chain-link fence and he can't remember the last time he did what he is about to do and, with an old-man sort of frog hop, Murray catches on to the fence and clambers up and gingerly over the top, and lowers himself down on the other side, where he turns to see that he is in a different city now. Not a city at all, really.

Murray pauses to catch his breath, then resumes running, which slows to a jog, which slows to a brisk walk. It's quiet now, no sound track here, and Murray sees why: he's on some kind of backstage lot, now, which he knows because he sees crews of men constructing sets and façades, making a town that looks like just the town Murray grew up in. Even more like the town he remembers: an imagined place more real than the place it is supposed to be. A designed substitute that destroys the memory of the original. Murray sees a sign that says

*Coming Soon*
(from AEI, the people who brought you
The Brad™):
**YOUR HOMETOWN**

and below it another sign that says "Re-Authenticization in Process" and below that, in minuscule type, a legal notice that the town is now owned by The American Experience, LLC, whose parent company, American Entertainments, Inc. (AEI), is a subsidiary itself of a company called The USAmusement Corporation, which is owned by a German conglomerate, New World Experiments GmbH, owned by a consortium led by Chinese and Korean investors. All around is new ground being broken, dig sites surrounded by chain-link fences, men working in hard hats, large colorful banners proclaiming that Your Hometown will be relaunched in the Fall of 2015.

Murray runs from door to door, looking for an exit from this place. It all looked so good in the brochures, but now he isn't sure where he is, doesn't know anymore what is real or not real, whether he really does have cancer or if that is just part of this, this whatever-it-is, experiential lifestyle product or whatever Rick, or whoever-he-is, called it. True, Murray had been looking for some kind of adventure, but this is not exactly what he had in mind, this manufactured situation, not a fantasy but a kind of trick of the mind, a trick of the heart. This is the same place, the town as advertised, not just a town with a lowercase "t" but a Town, the Town, the scene having been redone by the Tourism Bureau, quantified in the grand Re-Quaintification Initiative, a restoration of the town's rich history and tradition, which Murray now understands as just more advertising copy written by AEI. All of the buildings and street signs and lampposts and mailboxes, all of it décor, a set, a three-dimensional illusion, part physical, part digital, designed with the purpose of making Murray, or not Murray, the citizen of the town, the citizen of American Entertainments, Inc., a corporate-owned municipality, or citizen wasn't the right word—customer—all of it designed to make the customer a tourist in his own hometown. A hometown that he never really grew up in, one that never even existed. Everything that had seemed comforting about it before, the ornate overhangs, the stained wood porches, the restaurant signs with all of the charming fonts all serving chicken fingers, all of it now seems off.

Murray is in an empty theme park, an hour before it opens, not quite ready to be the place it is supposed to be.

Or perhaps a deserted back lot, an abandoned set for one of those network shows, with all of the mopey people in large houses, being sad at each other. *That's it,* Murray realizes, although he isn't quite sure what he is realizing, it is more like the feeling of realizing something, which people in those shows tend to do much more often than in actual life.

Murray tries another door and finally one opens, and now he's running up what appears to be some kind of corporate office disguised as part of the town. The elevator door is open and lit and appears to be waiting for Murray, which gives Murray the creeps and he thinks it might be best, if this is some kind of story planned out for him, if this is all part of The Brad™, that maybe he should avoid that elevator, if he's going to have any chance of getting out of here. Plus, Murray can hear music coming out of that elevator, and not just any music, but the same music heard before, *the sound track,* his sound track or the sound track to Autumn®, thundering major-chord tonality, the melody seeming to physically lift something inside Murray, lifting him up and drawing him toward the elevator, and Murray wonders if somehow the song has been engineered to fit him, based on some kind of preference matrix, to suit his emotional and psychological makeup, to push his invisible buttons, buttons he didn't even realize he had until he heard this music, and Murray knows that he can't get in the elevator. He opens the door marked "Exit" and goes through it and sees, a moment too late, that it isn't an exit, now he is in the stairwell and the door has shut behind him. He tries it. Locked. He shakes it with all of his strength, waning now, he's tired, but gives it a good shake and kicks the handle a few times for good measure, but knows he has no choice but to go up the stairs, probably up to wherever the elevator was going to take him anyway. He has been fooled, he sees, trying to avoid the elevator, the choice he thought that they wanted him to take, and now he has taken the choice that they wanted him to take anyway. *I'm losing it,* Murray thinks. *They? Who are they?* And just when Murray thinks he might be paranoid, he hears the sound track, faint, coming from up above, the sound falling down the stairwell, getting louder as he climbs each flight. He checks each floor of this empty, fake building, knowing that he will end up on the roof, because that's where *they* want him to go. The music is getting louder and the feeling is getting stronger, stronger in proportion to the volume of the sound track, the feeling that Murray is realizing something. *What has come over me?* Murray wonders, and it occurs to him that searching frantically for an exit is perhaps exactly what someone in Murray's situation would be expected to do. That's what Murray has been doing all his life. Getting up when the alarm goes off. Going to work. Coming straight home from work. A drink or three in the evening, and do it all over again. Straight ahead, plodding along with the plot. And now he has signed up for more of the same, wanting a little taste of what other people had, lured in by the promise of two bedrooms and two bathrooms with shiny fixtures and baskets of individually wrapped soaps, all of the shiny products just part of the larger one, the largest one, a way of life, life itself as a product. This is what he has always wanted, or so he had thought, but now here he is, in the middle of a story of his own and looking for the exit, and realizing all the exits are blocked and then realizing that an exit is not what he needs. Why should he leave? He, for once, is the center of the story, and for the first time in as long as he can remember, Murray feels that he is in control. This is it: his all-time high point. The apex of his trajectory, his moment of total freedom, the moment that Murray has been waiting for his whole life. To feel completely free and real and himself. An authentic experience. *This is my real self,* Murray thinks, but almost as soon as he thinks it, he wonders, who is deciding that? Himself, or some self separate from the self, and what is an authentic experience if you realize it as such while still having it? Now that Murray has labeled it as authentic, could it still be that? *Who is putting these ideas into my head?* And he wonders if they are even his own ideas or somehow part of The Brad™, part of some kind of dramedic consciousness, an internal voice-over, that the product engineers at American Entertainments, Inc., have come up with a way to make him understand his own life as a kind of story. *Is that it?* Murray wonders, and as he reaches the top of the stairwell and throws open the roof access door, Murray thinks, *yes, that's right, you've got it,* and he realizes that he didn't think that last thought, *no you didn't, Murray, that was me,* and he sees Rick standing up on top of the ledge of the building, six stories up, and he says, *hey Murray,* and Murray realizes Rick is somehow *narrating directly into Murray's head.*

"Stop that," Murray screams.

"Oh fine," Rick says.

"How did you get up here?" Murray says between gulps of air.

"You thought it would be that easy to get rid of me?"

"Kind of, yeah."

"Don't you see? You can't escape your arc."

"My life isn't an arc," Murray says. "I've figured it out."

"That so? Tell me."

"I'm not fighting it anymore," Murray says.

"Go on," Rick says, with a smile. "I'm listening." He hands Murray a handkerchief to wipe his forehead.

Murray takes it and dries off, wiping his face and neck. "I made a break for it during the commercial," Murray says, after catching his breath.

"Yup."

"I heard the music in the elevator, so I took the stairs."

"Yes, yes."

"By resisting your story, I was actually creating it for you."

Rick looks a little surprised. "Pretty good," he says. "Really good, actually. Hardly anyone ever figures that out.

But let me ask you a question: what are you going to do now?"

"I've still got seven days to change my mind."

"This is true," Rick says. "But let me show you something."

Rick pulls a small ring box out of his pocket and opens it to reveal a small toggle switch.

"What is that?" Murray says.

"The on-off switch."

"To what?"

"Why don't you flip it and find out?"

As soon as Murray hits the switch, he is deafened by a horrible grinding sound. From out of nowhere Rick produces two sets of earphones. He hands one to Murray and puts the other pair on himself.

"Ah, that's better," says Rick. "Can you hear me?"

Murray nods, unsure of how he feels with Rick once again talking right into his head, but then he sees where the grinding is coming from.

"I'll give you a moment," Rick says, as he watches Murray take in what he's looking at, which is the same town he was just running through, the Town, only now it's not empty, but filled with workers in orange jumpsuits. From behind false walls and through false doors, men appear in twos and threes, wearing blue jackets that say "CONTINU-ITY" on the back, armed with pressurized canisters and fine brushes.

"That stuff is called RealLife™," Rick says. "Aerosolized Themed Ambience."

Rick and Murray watch as the men descend upon threadbare corners of the room, holes in the scene where the wire frame is showing through, or the substrate, or whatever was underneath, expertly applying coats and touch-ups to blank patches of reality, surgical and precise with their movements, smoothing over, restoring, stitching the illusion back together, and then, just as quickly as they appeared, the Continuity maintenance workers disappear.

"Where are we?" Murray says.

"Backstage," Rick says.

The next wave of workers appears, in purple jumpsuits, with white lettering on the back that reads "DISCONTI-NUITY," and Murray watches as they appear to undo some of the work that was just done by their predecessors in Continuity, selectively erasing certain bits of the landscape, scuffing a corner here, rubbing away a bit of reality there. Rick explains to Murray that these guys are actually from a completely different department than Continuity.

"It's part of Accounts Receivable," Rick says.

If a customer doesn't keep current on payments of the Continuity Maintenance Fee for The Brad™ or The Jake™ or whatever other product they may have chosen, then corporate calls in the continuity disruption team to initi-ate the Experience Degradation Ladder.

"Like repo men," Murray says. "For the life I bought."

"Now you're catching on," Rick says. "Look at all that. It's a beautiful thing." Murray tries to see what Rick is talking about, but all he sees is a kind of factory. A manufacturing process for a way of life. Taking anything, experience, a piece of experiential *stuff,* a particle of particularity, a sound, a day, a song, a bunch of stuff that happens to people, a thing that makes you laugh, a visual, a feeling, whatever. A mess. A blob. A chunk. A messy, blobby, chunky glob of stuff. Unformed, raw noncontent that gets engineered, honed, and refined until some magical point where it has been processed to sufficient smoothness and can be extruded from the machine: content. A chunk of content, homogeneous and perfect for slicing up into Content Units. All of this for the customer-citizens, who demand it, or not even demand it but come to expect it, or not even expect it, as that would require awareness of any alternative to the substitute, an understanding that this was not always so, that, once upon a time, there was the real thing. They don't demand it or expect it. They assume it. The product is not a product, it's built into the very notion of who they are. Content Units everywhere, all of it coming from the same source: jingles, news, ads. Ads, ads, ads. Ads running on every possible screen. Screens at the grocery store, in the coffee line, on the food truck, in your car, on top of taxis, on the sides of buses, in the air, on the street signs, in your office, in the lobby, in the elevator, in your pocket, in your home. Content pipelines productive as ever, churning and chugging, pumping out the content day and night, conceptual smokestacks billowing out content-manufacturing waste product emissions, marginal unit cost of content dropping every day, content just piling up, containers full, warehouses full, cargo ships full, the channels stuffed to bursting with content. So much content that they needed to make new markets just to find a place to put all of it, had to create the Town, and after that, another Town, and beyond that, who knew? What were the limits for American Entertainments, Inc., and its managed-narrative experiential lifestyle products? How big could the Content Factory get?

"You brought me up here to see this?" Murray says.

"No," Rick says, "I brought you up here to see that."

Murray looks down to see his son getting out of his car.

"He's here to see you," Rick says. "He heard you're ... "

"Let me guess," Murray says. "Cancer."

"The doctors say you've got six months. But with modern medicine, who knows? You might live happily ever after. Or at least, happily enough."

"Your doctors? In here? TV doctors?"

"They're the best in the world. They also have very complicated love lives."

"I'm not even sick," Murray says.

"Are you sure about that?"

"Is that, are you, is that some kind of threat?"

"No, no no, noooo. Murray, come on. I'm not a bad guy. I'm not your antagonist. I'm just here to give you choices."

Murray looks down again and sees his son, someone or something that looks exactly like his son. Except that something seems off.

"Wait a minute," Murray says. "Is that even my real son?"

"Depends on how you define real," Rick says. "Are you sure you're still the real Murray?"

Murray doesn't even know what that means, but he is tired of this sales guy messing with his head and it seems to Murray that the absolute right thing to do, or perhaps absolute wrong thing to do, or perhaps the absolute right thing to do because it is the absolute wrong thing to do, or just in terms of what will feel good, would be to punch Rick or "Rick" or whatever right in that smug mouth of his, so Murray plants a foot, puts his weight into it as best he knows how, and pops Rick right in that very real mouth of his, flesh and bone on flesh and teeth and that, Murray is sure, is something solid and visceral and real, and Rick goes down.

"Wow," Rick says, still lying on the ground, hand covering his mouth, blood running onto his gums and fingers.

"Sorry," Murray says, shocked by what he's done. "I guess I watch too much TV."

"No no no," Rick says. "Happens to me all the time. It's a good way to end your story. Something tangible, decisive, action-oriented."

"I was supposed to hit you?" Murray says, coming to see what that means. "I can't escape my arc."

Rick nods, like a proud teacher. "You're not going to live forever. Everyone has their time, of course, but if you stay in here, it'll be dramatic, and meaningful, and all of that good stuff," Rick says, pointing down at Murray's son or "son" or whatever. "And as you can see, you won't be alone. This is what it comes down to, Murray. If you stay in here, you get closure. If you leave, well, I don't know what happens to you out there."

*What am I going to do now?* Murray thinks, now realizing that he really is having his epiphany: he is free. Completely free. This is his big Change of Life scene. All his life he's been waiting. But even now as it is happening, as he tries to hold on to it, it is slipping from him, a shell, just the diaphanous skin of an epiphany, which, with the softest whisper, slips off and floats into the air, the form of the experience, without the substance, the husk of a moment. It feels false. A false resolution. Closure. This is what Rick is offering: a sound-tracked life. Life as a story. A story as a product. *Is this really the best he can hope for? Is this all there is?*

*Shut up*, Murray thinks to himself. *Just shut the hell up and stop narrating to yourself. Shut up shut up shut up shut up. Shut up.*

And then it's quiet. The factory is gone. Rick is gone. The music is gone. Even Murray's own internal monologue is gone. Behind Murray is his backstory, his life. In front of him is who knows what. But how does he just go on now, having seen what he's seen? The guts of it. The gears. The machinery of production of his reality. His existence as a customer. As a paying customer in a managed lifestyle experience. This is what it is, what it has been for some time now. The only difference is that now he knows it. Murray has chosen The Brad™ but it's not enough, or it's too much, or neither or both. His life is not a dramedy.

There is no arc. No episodes, no tuning in next week, no sound track, no ending, happy or sad. He may or may not have cancer. He may or may not have anyone who cares. He has a son in the world, somewhere, who might or might not think of Murray every day. Not much else. Not enough for a story, Murray thinks, here at the edge of his own story, but it will have to do, somehow it's going to have to be enough, and somehow it is. It's enough.

All of the Above

## Sorry Please Thank You

You're reading this, so it's too late. For me, I mean. I'm gone. That's redundant, isn't it? What the hell am I doing—only so much space on this napkin and I'm using it up on rhetorical questions? What a metaphor for life—a finite space, impossibly small. No way to fit a whole lifetime in there. But we sure do try. Oh God, I am annoying. I even annoy myself. I'm out of control with this kind of stuff, I know. This is why you never really loved me. Got one bullet in the chamber, barrel jammed in waistband, metal cold against my skin. One bullet, one napkin. Napkin that my last drink was sitting on. Jameson, rocks. Running out of space, so I'll start to get to the point:

You said I'd get over it.

Should have made you a bet, because, hey, guess what, got a loaded gun in my underwear so it turns out I was right. Not that I can complain. Had some good years. My life, nutshell: 0–8 yrs. happy, no reason; 9–19 happy, wrong reasons; 20–33 unhappy for all the right reasons; 34 to present moment, unhappy, looking for a reason. Sorry, man. I get that a lot. I'm sorry for your loss, people say to one another. What does that mean? I wish it weren't so. I can imagine a world in which it had not happened. But that's not what sorry means. Sorry means: That happened to you. That happened to you and it may or may not have been inevitable, but it happened and there are some things that happen that we can only look at and say, sorry. Circular. Sorry for your loss means I am sorry that there is loss, or to put it another way, there is loss. The sorry cancels itself out, and it might only mean this: that happened to you, and I can see that it hurt, and I am going to say this word, sorry, that corresponds to something, a vector, a medium of propagation and/or force-carrying particle that allows transmission or communication of sorrow, or the related but not identical state of sorryness, a mysterious action-at-a-distance between humans that allows one human, separated in space and time from another human, to impart upon the other an influence, an effect. The state of being sorry.

What else can I say? Wish I'd treated people better. Sorry, please, thank you, you're welcome. All human interaction pretty much covered by those four ideas. You're not real, of course. You're the woman I wish I'd met. If I'd met you, I wouldn't be here now, writing on this napkin. You're the woman who was supposed to pull me out of this, help me get over the one I did lose. So, yeah, a little angry. How does a perfectly average-looking guy like me end up so unfathomably lonely by the age of forty-one? It's the day after Christmas. Got one present this year, from my uncle Jim. The widower. A card and a ten-dollar bill. Fixed income, best he can do. He's in assisted living, room smells like pee. Stares out the window all day. Every year, same gift. I'm a grown man now, but I'm his only nephew and he's my only family. I'm leaving it on the bar as a tip. The card, I'm keeping. Sorry, get well, congratulations. Happy belated. Miss you. Just because. The fundamentals, the basics, all right there, in your drugstore, the greeting card rack. If you'd only said it, if you'd only had one more chance to say it. If someone had said to me. Any of it. I hope you read this, whoever you are, and imagine that there is a hypothetical person out there who needs your love, has been waiting silently, patiently for it all his life, is flawed and downright ugly at times and yet would have just eaten up any tiny bit of attention you had been willing to give, had you ever stopped your own happy life to notice. And then imagine that this hypothetical person is real, because he probably is. Guess that's all. Ha. Here I was worrying about space, and now I've run out of things to say. Wish I knew a joke to insert HERE. The card says For My Nephew in cursive. No joke inside. That cursive just breaks my heart. Wish I'd met you. Wish I wasn't your hypothetical. But you're reading this, which means a few minutes ago, I went into that bathroom and pulled the trigger. You probably heard it. Sorry. You're welcome. Thank you. And please. Please, please, please, please, please, please, please.

## Acknowledgments

☑ **THANK YOU,** and also +2d6 coins (redeemable for a whole chicken):

- ☐ Timothy O'Connell
- ☐ Josefine Kals
- ☐ Kate Runde
- ☐ Alexander Houstoun
- ☐ Russell Perrault
- ☐ Edward Kastenmeier
- ☐ Dan Frank
- ☐ Catherine Courtade
- ☐ Kathleen Fridella
- ☐ Altie Karper
- ☐ Peter Mendelsund
- ☐ All of the other talented people at Pantheon and Vintage/Anchor. It is a privilege to work with you.

☑ **PLEASE** accept my +100 debits of Gratitude™, an electronic transfer system for appreciation:

- ☐ Gary Heidt
- ☐ Howard Sanders

☐ Jason Richman

☐ Arthur Spector

☐ Amy Grace Loyd

☐ John Joseph Adams

☐ Ann VanderMeer

☐ Jeff VanderMeer

☐ Rich Horton

☐ Carol Ann Fitzgerald

☐ Marc Smirnoff

☐ Jonathan Liu

☐ Marian Leitner

☐ Annalee Newitz

☐ Charlie Jane Anders

☐ Tom Chiarella

☑ **SORRY** for not saying this more often: Thank you. Please know how much you have given me.

☐ Betty Yu

☐ Jin Yu

☐ Kelvin Yu

☐ Dylan ☐ Sophia

☐ Michelle